Surfing for Wayan

Surfing for Wayan

Steve Tolbert's other young adult books are

Channeary
Settling South
Stepping Back
Eyeing Everest
Escape to Kalimantan
Tracking the Dalai Lama
Dreaming Australia
Packing Smack, Talking Wombats
O'Leary, JI Terrorist Hunter

For further information go to www.southcom.com.au/~stolbert

Steve Tolbert

Surfing for Wayan

& other stories

Thank you
Tansy Rayner Roberts, Lynley Hocking,
Steven 'Heathen' Clark and Tamzen Roberts

Surfing for Wayan & other stories
ISBN 978 1 740271 353 4
Copyright © text Steve Tolbert 2006
Text drawings: Tamzen Roberts
Cover: Helen Poynter

First published 2006
Reprinted 2016

GINNINDERRA PRESS
PO Box 3461 Port Adelaide 5015
www.ginninderrapress.com.au

Contents

2002 BALI BOMBING
MEMORIAL, JL, LEGIAN, KUTA

Surfing for Wayan

Right, this is what's going through my head. I'm sitting here watching the Medewi point surf because of seven people. Four are dead. Three are alive. Of the three who are alive, Agung is around the corner at the warung.* Mum is back home in Hobart fretting and SMS-reminding me to stay out of Bali's tourist areas. And the last person, Made,‡ is fast becoming my main reason for doing that. She's sitting next to me, posture-perfect, using her right hand as a sun visor and watching the surf also. If anything good has come from the ache of the past four years, it's meeting up with her and her father again in Bangli and coming here.

I should be out there in the three-metre surf instead of bum-bound to this dinosaur egg of a rock, my surfing plans on hold, my voice quaky, my skin all tingly and warm. Yesterday, at Nusa Dua, I was the picture of centrefold surfer cool studying the break, working out the rips, getting my wetsuit on and rubbing a ten-year supply of wax over my board while eyeing off Made standing next to her father. I got in the water – eventually. But today she's sitting closer to me than any girl ever has before. The tide's dropping. Her thin, long-fingered hand's occupying the small space between us. A breeze has come up, rippling the water. My eyes are double-edged magnets flicking from her to the surf, before settling on her again. She catches me, and smiles into my eyes. I grin back, feeling my ears shift. If I don't get out in the surf soon, there'll be nothing survivable to get out there for. And that's why I'm back in Bali, supposedly – to surf big time, for everybody, everyday.

'Big waves when you surf here before, Jacob?' Made asks.

I wish I could say, No, Made, nothing over seven or eight metres. Big

* open food stall
‡ pronounced Ma-day

brother Joey would have. Thinking of him sends my roller coaster mood plummeting again.

'No,' I truth-tell. 'But at the time they looked like mountains to me. I was scared and couldn't surf much.' I feel suddenly breathless, like I've just popped my head up above water after almost drowning, which ignites another memory.

***

'Aerodynamic speed fin perfection,' Joey shouted out four years ago, racing up the sand with his board after another surf mag spell in the Clifton surf. 'More lift, more hold, less drag, less load: looser, smoother, turbo-powered spiral tube mover.' He stopped, puffing hard, and thrust Quiksilver at me. 'Your ticket to surfing heaven. Go on, do it, Jakeman, do it! Chuck out the kiddies' board and tie on to Quiksilver. It doesn't get any better than this.'

To stop him pestering me, I did it, finally, paddling his board out towards the surf line for the first time ever.

'Eh, it's the Jakeman, ready to walk on water,' Rap welcomed me, further out.

Big-eyed Fish looked around lazily, giving me the thumbs up, before turning his attention back out to sea. 'Tsunami! Tsunami!' he screamed minutes later, as I gazed towards shore. He and Rap were paddling hard towards a huge, lifting wave that looked intent on swamping the sun. 'Paddle, Jakeman! Paddle!'

Panic-struck, I flattened myself to the board and dug my arms in the water faster than I ever thought possible, urging myself to get over that great, rising mass of water before it crashed down, burying me.

Seconds later, Rap and Fish streaked up the wave's face, clearing it in a rainbow of fine spray, their boards slapping down on the other side.

'Whoohhh there, cowboy!' Rap yelled, unseen.

Then it was on me. I could only hang on shooting up its face, then slowing and curling back over as it collapsed in an avalanche roar, hurling me down into an explosion of water and violent jerks. I couldn't escape the weight of water pressing me down – my chest and throat shot with pain, blood thudding in my ears, my strength gone – before the distant hum of a voice came. Hands gripped my wrists and yanked, and I popped up into blurred sunlight, gasping and sucking away at the sweet air.

That voice came again, close and clear. 'Arms over the board, Fish.'

Rap shouted, 'That's it. That's it.'

'I'll get his legs.'

'Jake!' Joey was on my boogie board, his hands cradling my head. 'Jake! Jake! You gotta' hear me! You got to!'

'I hear you,' I said, with great effort. My stomach surged. I tried to jerk my head away, but Joey's grip was too tight. I spewed over his hands and arms then took in more air hanging there limp, side-on across Quiksilver and vowing never again to get on a surfboard.

***

'You do not look scared now.' Made's voice brings me back. Her eyes are dark brown bubbles, still and soft.

Clueless about what to say next, I go into two-word reply mode. 'Don't I?' Joey would have spouted an entire page from *Rip Curl* magazine in the time it takes for me to say that.

She shakes her head, fingering strands of hair back behind her ear. How long would I have to know her, I ask myself, before offering to do that for her?

'You go in the surf soon?' she asks.

I pick up a stone and toss it towards the water where there're about fifty million others. For a moment, I wonder if she wants to be alone. But that's not the message her eyes and mouth are sending. 'Yeah, soon.'

She stands, tilting her head and raising her eyebrows at me. 'You want a drink?'

'No thanks.' I watch her turn and cross the rocks – thongs flapping, tight Hard Rock T-shirt and jeans gripping, her hair like black silk flowing down her back. Maybe if I wait long enough, a shark fin will show out there and give me an excuse to ask her for a walk along the beach, like for the rest of the day. It's not the first time I've thought up excuses for opting out of the Medewi surf. The dark lines of another set are building up out there. Half a dozen surfers – three more than last time I was here, packing death – are positioning themselves for the steep A-frame take-offs. Watching them, I think of Dad and the press of memory grips me again.

***

Everything Dad felt could be read in his smiles: his people-recognition and fatherly smiles of concern and protection in the early days, then his dazed smile, born of excruciating pain and despair after he fell off his mate Benny's ladder, broke his back and never came right again. Finally, the tear-glazed, dwelling-on-Joey smile he wore when we were here back in 2002. 'If your old man ever entered a smile pageant, Jake boy,' Benny said to me once, before Dad's fall, 'I'd bet the house, the car and my wife's false teeth he'd win it. Like a burst of bright light that big, boofhead grin of his is when he first lays eyes on me. It's like seeing me is the best part of his day. Your old man could stop wars with that smile.'

The problem was that nothing could stop the war going on in his head after his fall. He and Mum split up and he fled south to live in a bush caravan out the back of Woodbridge. Nothing helped him down there. Not the solitude and quiet. Not Knuckles, the small, stray dog that adopted him before becoming mine. Not me offering to go down there and go surfing with him. Only the time he spent in The Mermaid's front bar seemed capable of giving him any relief, temporarily.

My thoughts wander to that worst of all mornings.

Joey and Fish were in Bali, and I was at the computer booking tickets for the Jack Johnson concert, like Joey asked me to. Mum, at the dining table, turned on the radio news. The ABC's signal music sounded. 'Tragedy engulfs Bali,' the newsreader exclaimed, as if he were there witnessing it. 'Terrorist bombing kills scores of people in Kuta Beach, including many Australians.'

We listened in stilled horror. Mum turned on the TV and we watched news updates for an hour before she rang the Bali Bombing hotline. After that, action wilted to waiting again – by the phone and computer – for Joey to make contact and assure us they were all right. The phone rang, but only relatives or friends or Fish's parents were on the other end.

'No,' mum replied. 'We haven't heard from Joey yet. But Indonesia's a poor country. Phones and computers can't be easy to access, especially with what's happened.' Then, faking it in upbeat mode, she repeated to people – and afterwards to me as though she were practising for the next caller – how small the chances were that Joey and Fish had been in those places when the bombs went off.

Despair thickened in the intervals before the phone rang again, jarring us into renewed hope.

'No, Joey hasn't rung up yet, but…'

I let Mad Dog in. He plopped down in his beanbag and slept and snored. The wind chime tinkled on the veranda. Inside, the wall clock beat the time without Bali contact, and the chances grew that Joey and Fish had been in Paddy's Bar or The Sari Club.

'I suppose I'd better try to get in touch with your father,' Mum said at midday, staring at the floor. She rang his mobile. It was turned off. 'Typical,' she said, before leaving a message.

The phone stayed quiet. Nothing came through on the computer. News footage showed The Sari Club in flames – red and blue lights flashing, the street a mirror of watery reflections. Westerners milled about – scorched, horrified, their clothes hanging off them. We stretched forward and searched the screen.

Towards tea time the phone rang. I answered it. Voices and laughter and the jangle of gaming machines competed in the background. Dad's grim voice didn't fit in with what was going on around him.

Mum's expression turned hard as she took the phone and told him what she knew, which didn't take long.

Forty minutes later, the engine rumble and brake squeal of Dad's EH Holden sounded outside. When his car door slammed, Mum went to the door and opened it, seemingly undecided whether to let him in or not. Finally, she walked away and he stepped in with half a dozen stubbies under his arm.

'Hi ya,' he mumbled to me, not expecting an answer. He sat on the sofa beside me, opened a stubby and gazed at the television screen.

Mum and I stayed quiet. Mad Dog snored.

Dad drank his stubbies through a series of news updates. Finished, he got up and moved to the computer. 'Right. I'm going up there to find him, or at least find out what's happened to him. Anyone else coming?'

'No,' Mum answered quickly.

'I want to.'

Her angry glare made me feel traitorous. 'No, absolutely not, Jacob.'

'Please, Mum.'

'He's a big boy, Mary,' Dad intervened, boldly. 'He'll be a big help. I've got the money to get him up there if he thinks it's important enough to…'

'The money you've yet to drink up, you mean?' All her pent-up emotion spilled out as she honed into him about the usual things. 'And you stand there spouting your sanctimonious bullshit about what's important for him.'

Mad Dog woke and scampered to the door.

'One son's missing, Tom, I'm not eager to lose my other one.'

'Neither am I,' he said evenly. 'I'll look after him.'

'You can't look after yourself.' She jumped up as if wasp-stung and marched to the door. 'I just can't believe you.' She let Mad Dog out and kept on going.

***

Made's back, prompting a mood change. She sits down and offers me her drink can. I take a swig. 'Father says we can go if you not want to surf here,' she tells me.

Four years ago, he said the same thing about a place called Soka, just down the road from here. I look down at the rock edge between my outspread legs and remember Dad sitting here, swigging away on his Bintang pain killers. 'No one's holding a gun to your head,' he said to me then.

'Of all the places I've planned to surf in Bali,' I say to Made, passing her drink can back, 'Medewi is the most important to me.'

'Always for Wayan too,' she says.

I know that, and tell her so. Older brothers, no longer around, are what we share. 'Time to surf,' I say to myself, giving in to my supposed purpose for being here. I decide against wearing my wetsuit and reach for the sun cream. As I spread it on exposed body parts, she watches.

When I get to my back, and start stretching like a contortionist, she extends her hand, palm up, and says, 'Want me?'

Yes. You wouldn't believe how much, I think, before passing her the cream. 'Thanks.'

She starts rubbing it in slowly, like I'm not due to get in the water until tomorrow.

'More?' she asks too soon.

'Yes.' I scan the water looking for that shark fin. It still doesn't show.

With a ten-year supply of sun protection on my back, I finally grab Quiksilver and paddle out. In the lull between sets, I sit up and look back at Made. My mind flashes back to the day I first saw her wearing a golden headdress, her hands clasped in front of her face, a big tear sliding down her cheek.

***

Broken window glass crunched underfoot as I walked across Joey's hotel room to a bedside table with travel brochures and an itinerary, written in his HSC Indonesian, strewn over it. 'Bali. All you could imagine…and more' the caption on the top brochure read. I'd seen it before. Filling up the rest of that glossy page were tropical flowers, scuba-diving Westerners, batik clothing and terraced rice fields. I dropped the brochures and itinerary on top of the other things in Joey's bag.

Only two things remained, which was fortunate, as Dad's back pain and the sorrow and the heavy heat were weighing us down. Dad moved over to the blown-out window and looked down at Poppie's Lane.

'Surfboard and board bag too? I asked him.

'Everything goes, Jacob. If you can get his board down the steps, I'll carry the bag as far as the reception desk. I'd like to take one more walk along the main road. You don't have to come if you don't want to.'

'I'm coming.'

In the three days we searched the Kuta area, it's what Dad always said before we started wandering off in a different direction, or hopped into another

13

bemo to go to another chaotic, casualty-packed hospital. And after running out of places to search, and determining where Joey had to be, we toured the bombsite over and over again.

At the reception desk, Dad took out Joey's itinerary and slipped it into his back pocket before we stepped into Poppie's Lane, turned right and began winding past the debris and blank-faced people coming the other way.

On Jalan Legian, we headed towards the bombsite: the giant crater-covering tent, the stacks of rubble, burnt-out cars and skeletal buildings. Casually dressed Western investigators sifted through the destruction. They outnumbered the Indonesian policemen, whose crisply pressed uniforms seemed better suited to a parade ground than a disaster site. In what was once the middle of the road, there was a huge, white cross, surrounded by wreaths, photos and messages. An eerie quiet persisted, as if the street's quota for noise and destruction had been expended in the bomb blast. Just the intermittent sounds of rubble being shifted and a few muffled voices before we heard chanting coming from the shade of a burnt-out vehicle to our left.

Catching the sweet smell of incense, we stepped to one side and viewed a group of traditionally dressed Balinese sitting cross-legged around a small shrine of rice and water and yellow flower petals. Their eyes were lowered in prayer and they held glowing incense sticks between clasped palms. One girl, maybe thirteen or fourteen, wore a golden headdress adorned with pink flowers. Her eyes were closed, and she held her head higher than the others and was the only one in the circle not chanting. A big, pearl-like tear slid down her face to her cheek, where it stopped as if snap-frozen.

'Transport?' asked a thin, middle-aged man sitting on the step of what once was the Aloha Surf Shop. When no one replied, he gazed back down at his feet.

Dad glanced from the driver to the chanters to the cross on the road, before taking out Joey's itinerary. 'Have you ever used your brother's surfboard, Jacob?'

Joey, acclaimed Quiksilver surf king, I thought. Me, one go and nearly drowned before even reaching the surf; ever since relegated to my 'kiddies' board'. It wasn't a story I wanted to share. 'No,' I lied, feeling my face flush.

'Anybody's?

'No.'

His dazed eyes stayed on me. 'After tonight, I don't think there's anything more we can do here in Kuta. But I do think we can do one more thing for Joey. So what about this? We put our flight on hold for a few days and email your mother to explain why. Then in the morning we get a boogie board and some fins from somewhere, take along Joey's board as well, and head off surfing.'

'Where?' I asked, pretty certain I knew.

He read a few places off Joey's itinerary then added, 'And anywhere else you think you'd like to surf for your brother.'

I looked down at my feet like that driver bloke was doing. It wasn't the heat or sorrow, but the pressure of expectation that weighed on me. At some point, the suggestion would have to come that I start using Quiksilver to surf. 'Do you think it's safe for us to do that?' I asked, hoping he'd change his mind.

'Why don't I go over and ask the bloke on the step? I reckon he'll tell us.'

While Dad did that, the chanting continued and that girl sat statue-still, the track of her tear drying pale to her cheek.

***

She's sitting perfectly still now, though her appearance has changed heaps since that day. Girls used to sit on Clifton Beach and look out at Joey, Rap and Fish too, while I, the group mascot, boogie boarded in the wash close to shore.

I like the feeling of Made watching me now – well, watching me while most likely thinking about Wayan. But that's fine. Like Joey, he was obviously someone to live up to. I wish I'd met him.

Turning, I spot the next set before the others do and paddle into the peak position. A couple of quick strokes and I'm on. I snap turn and tuck into a gaping, dry-hole tube – the thrill sending my skin electric – before I run out of wave and flick out. I head back out past the break, where I sit up and think about the last time I was here.

***

'I'm Tom.' It was the first word out of anyone since we drove off from Kuta in the bemo half an hour earlier. Dad motioned towards the back seat just as another big hotel showed up on our right. 'And this is my son, Jacob.'

Security guards were suddenly everywhere.

'I am Agung.' Our driver volunteered nothing more.

'Like Gunung Agung, the volcanic mountain of the gods?' Dad asked.

'Yes, like that.' Agung turned off down a dirt track. 'Many places you can surf at Nusa Dua,' he said, 'but today Sri Lanka break best place.' We rolled and bounced our way down to a small car park, empty except for a couple of dirt-crusted motorbikes with surfboard brackets on their sides.

After stopping and getting out, I grabbed my boogie board, while Agung reached for Joey's surfboard on the roof rack. 'You belly surf or real surf today?' he asked, tossing away his cigarette stub.

That stung. With an audience of at least two down there in the surf, there was no doubt which board I wanted to use. 'Maybe we could take both boards and see what the surf's like.' I prayed for it to be closed out so I could use the boogie board close in. But then, if I kept thinking that way, who'd do the so-called real surfing for Joey over the next three days? Not that it concerned Dad which board I used.

'Up to you,' Agung said, averting his eyes. 'Always right break here. Today I think only one metre — not so big, but still good until wind come.' His roof rack and knowledge of surfing conditions seemed strange for someone as old and tired-looking as him.

Descending the worn path, we watched swells build and hang like aqua glass, before toppling over and peeling off. Down on the beach, Dad told Agung who the surfboard belonged to and that I'd never ridden one before.

After he placed the board on the sand, Agung lit up another fag and blew out a plume of smoke, like his volcanic namesake. 'Enjoy boogie board,' he said. 'I wait in bemo.'

Heading west an hour later, villages and plant life finally took over from the traffic and fumes of the city. Distant mountains on our right grew colourless in the hazy afternoon light. Small estuaries and bays showed when the road

16

dipped suddenly, then up we went again into sunbeams and tree shadow and two-second views of nearby fields.

'That is good surfboard you have. Is Joey good surfer?' Agung asked Dad, prompting conversation for the first time.

'He was, yes.'

The word 'was' seemed lost on Agung. 'So maybe little brother learn to ride it?'

'Maybe. I don't know. You'll have to ask him.'

But Agung didn't. Minutes passed before he said, 'Soka close to village. On hill next to beach with black sand. Can see river. Very beautiful. If want, can stay in bungalow at Losmen Lalang-Linggah. I get you special price. And still time to surf.'

'Sound all right to you, Jacob?' Dad called out.

'Yeah, fine,' I lied, as cold pangs of fear started to spread through my stomach.

'Maybe want to try surfboard there,' Agung suggested. 'Gelombang tak berat.' He eyed me in the rear-view mirror. 'Waves very gentle.'

Why couldn't he just keep out of it? I thought then, resenting the pressure he was putting on me. I stared out the window wishing for an engine breakdown or a flat tyre. It didn't happen.

Tucked in amongst creeper-covered banyan trees, our small room at Lalang-Linggah contained two huge wooden beds with mosquito nets. The shower and toilet were outside, connected to the room by a flight of steep steps. Coming up those steps, I hit a protruding beam with the heel of my hand and screamed out in faked pain. Back inside, rubbing my skull, I warned Dad about the beam and added, 'I might give surfing a miss today.'

He had a Bintang in his hand. More were on the floor. 'Fine,' he said, more concerned about finishing off his first stubby for the day than what my surfing plans were.

We went into the rumah makan and Dad mentioned my head problem to Agung, who glanced over at me.

'Okay for Medewi tomorrow?' he asked. 'Or want to go back to Kuta?' His face was a mask, without expression.

'No,' Dad responded quickly, not looking at me. 'We want to go to Medewi, don't we, Jake?'

I stayed quiet, watching Agung nod.

'Okay. Medewi not so far,' he said. 'Only twenty-five kilometre. Long left break there. But have to surf early. Wind come later.'

Dad polished off more stubbies while we ate. After leaving, we went down a root-strangled track and wandered along the black sand beach. A group of naked boys took running leaps in the water and bounced up wiping their faces, shrieking and laughing. Further on, villagers dragged a net parallel to the beach, shouting out and laughing too.

We sat against a warm boulder and watched the sun drop, crinkling the sea orange.

'I'm happy we decided to do this,' Dad said, slurring a little, his dwelling-on-Joey smile showing.

I looked away. 'Me too, Dad.'

By our door the next morning was an offering of banana leaf, a burning incense stick, rice and yellow flower petals. Next to the offering was a small wreath made from pink hibiscus flowers.

After breakfast, we chugged back out onto the undulating road and passed old men herding ducks with bamboo poles long as fly rods, women with washing baskets balanced on their heads and bag-carrying school children waiting for transport. Further in, farmers and water buffalo – at opposite ends of wooden ploughs – worked the fields. And I wondered if those people, like the villagers on the beach the previous day, ever read newspapers or listened to news reports, if they'd ever heard of Jalan Legian or Kuta Beach or Paddy's Bar or the Sari Club?

Dad mentioned to Agung the offering and the wreath left on our doorstep.

'Yes,' Agung replied. 'Also there is one for Wayan.' He shoved a cassette into the player. Strange, high-pitched music – full of cymbal, xylophone, drum and gong sounds – ended any thought of further conversation.

The first time Dad and I saw Agung smile was on the sand of Medewi Beach after he hopped up on Joey's board. With his arms outstretched, and wearing overlarge clothes, he looked more like a jumpsuit pegged to a *clothesline than a Balinese driver doubling as a surfing instructor, but not for long. He dropped belly flat to the board and said, 'Always Wayan say to people who want to surf, one two, one two, satu dua, satu dua. Like this. Satu.' He grabbed the edges. 'Dua.' He hopped up again, knees creaking. 'Harus lancar. Have to be smooth. Wayan good speaking English. Like riding dolphin, he always say to people.'*

Agung took a quick breather, looking out to sea. 'Then when stand,' he went on, 'remember back foot for steering, then have to twist which way want to go. Like this.' He performed a mock right turn, then a left one, before flattening himself on the board again. 'So altogether like this.' Up he hopped, puffing from the exercise. 'One, two belok ke kanan, ke kiri, turn to right, to left. Like I do.' He eyed me again, smiling encouragement, and I wondered if he'd been sharing Dad's Bintang. 'I know easy to do on sand,' he admitted, 'but have to start somewhere, Wayan always say to people.'

'Who's Wayan?' Dad asked.

Agung's look turned distant. 'Wayan best surfing teacher in Bali.' He turned to me. 'You try now, okay?'

I did so, reluctantly, my heartbeat quickening as I flattened myself on Quiksilver. Memories flooded back.

'So what's it to be?' Dad asked after I stood up on the board. 'Surfboard, boogie board, or nothing at all?'

Agung lit up a fag and stared at the surf. No one else was out there.

'My stomach's feeling a bit off, Dad,' I said, a spasm of shame surging through me. 'I think I'll stick to boogie boarding today.'

***

The water's faded to an aqua colour. Barnacled rocks, waving small green banners of algae, are showing underneath me. I should get out. The others have. The quick-dropping tide will make the waves wall up and lose shape. It'll get dangerous.

Made – the focus of my confused thoughts – still hasn't moved. It's like she's ossified to the rock she's on. That's not a word I would have used around Joey – the wordsmith of wave talk. Even when riding waves, he wave talked, or shouted: the surf his stage, the rest of the surfing world his imagined audience, packing the beach just to see him. His 'Banzai!' could turn heads in the back row, as far away as the car park.

Well, banzai time will start soon if I decide to stay out here and go another wave or two.

Joey would have.

***

'Banzai Pipeline International, by gun surfer invitation only,' Joey shouted out, leaping up on Mum's waterbed one night. 'Falling tide. Rising reef. Last ride, only for the brave-hearted. And here it comes. Rolling thunder. Tube of the century. And I'm on. Snap turn, I'm swallowed. Death's riding shotgun, Jakeman. Bum down, toes over, my arms a spear pointing towards that distant mist rainbow, that golden port holed light. BANZAAAIII! And I'm through, Jakeman. The floodlight sun's on me. A thousand cameras too. Fists are pumpin'. Spectators are jumpin'. Opposition's slumpin'. Ooooee! Kelly Slater, you're history. In your next ten lifetimes, you'll not catch a bullet ride to match that.'

Pumped-up Joey, great at riding, even better at describing. He could have written all the surf articles for all the surfing photos ever published without ever having to leave the house.

Later that night he asked me, 'How much of the readies you got stored away in the bank, little brother?'

'About six hundred.'

'Right. Bali will take twice that. So what you do is borrow the rest from moneybags here. No dramas, Jake. It's only sitting around in some dark vault going mouldy. One day when you're older and you're flush, you can half-shout me a Bali trip. There'll never be a time I won't want to go.'

'I don't think Mum'll go for it.'

'It's only for ten days: four of 'em Saturdays and Sundays. Bring along your laptop library. There'll be no night surfing, and thirteen is a bit young for touring the grog parlours, even over there, so you can stay room-bound and study for hours. If you need a break, take a splash in the pool. There's sure to be some sweet young thing in moonlit drawstring bikini there to give you a

needed boost and something extra to think about. No better cure for winter fever than that, eh, Jakeman? I'll guarantee you'll love it. And I promise, boogie board or surfboard, it'll make no difference. Your comfort, your choice.'

'Thanks, but I know Mum won't like the idea.'

Joey's eyes narrowed in thought. 'Depends on how we put it to her. The thing is, do you like the idea? If you do and want to go, then we'll work out a strategy here and now to convince her.'

Strands of Mad Dog's hairs showed on the carpet. I stooped down and picked a few up. 'The thing is…it's getting towards the end of the year.' I wasn't game to look at Joey. 'Exams are coming up. I really shouldn't be missing out on any school.'

***

It's strange how places that were once terrifying change and become comfort zones. First memories of going to bed at night and not wanting the light turned off, of dark alleyways steeped in playground horror stories now short cuts to the library and park, of being caught in a monster wave and almost drowning. Nowadays, straddling Quiksilver and thinking about that Clifton tsunami coming again is as much a part of my private world as reading books and writing stories.

And while waiting for it, I love bobbing on the surf-line like this, eyeing the reflections and listening to the quiet sounds you only notice out here – well, until the next set hits, anyway. And I surf well, I think.

'Joey ought to see you now, Jakeman,' Rap shouted out, with a thumbs-up sign of approval, while we were surfing at Roaring Beach last month. Luckily, he was too far away to see the effect that had on my eyes.

'Yeah, Rap,' I mumble, thinking about that day. I can almost touch the rocks with my feet now. Surfers have gathered in front of the warung. They're talking and glancing out here, and I imagine them saying something like, He must have bricks for a brain. When that next set hits, he'll be rock meat.

A minute later, Agung appears. He moves slowly over to Made. They talk and look out here as well, and I wonder, is it me they're seeing, or

Wayan? Wayan, I reckon. Predictably, Agung lights up a fag before sitting down where I sat earlier, where Dad sat the day I took Quiksilver out, packing death, for a second try.

***

Dad stood outside the open doorway and watched Agung drive off past the other thatched-roofed units. 'He's returning soon to take us into Negara,' Dad said. 'We can have a walk around then get something to eat there.'

The brief downpour had dwindled to a few spits of rain. A mass of brown-purple cloud moved out to sea. Moments later, the sun broke through.

I sat on my bed, beside a mound of mosquito netting with more fist-sized holes in it than material, and started scouring through my backpack for the mossie coils and matches.

Dad came in and plopped down on the end of his bed. 'While you were in the water this morning, I asked Agung about that bloke Wayan he talks so much about.'

'The best surfing teacher in all of Bali, you mean?' I found what I was after and placed the coil at the foot of our beds and lit it.

'Yes, him. Bali's best surfing teacher and also Agung's son. Same age as Joey, apparently.'

'Right,' I said, not surprised. 'So where's Wayan now?'

'The same place as Joey…more or less, give or take a few metres.' Dad ignored my reaction. 'Wayan worked at the Aloha Surf Shop. He and Agung took tourists on surfing trips. Some Australians contacted Wayan late on that Saturday night about wanting to tour the next day. He decided to open up the shop and was getting the necessary gear ready when the bomb exploded at Paddy's Bar next door. He must have run outside, like so many others did… When the big one went off, he…'

'Oh Jesus… So with the wreath at our door and all, Agung must know about Joey.'

'Yes. Once he knew who the surfboard belonged to, it didn't take much for him to work out what we're doing and why. I think in his mind, he's doing something similar… So how's the stomach feeling?'

22

'Okay.'

'Ready for some snorkeling then tomorrow?'

'Yeah, all right.'

The fan circled. Smoke spiralled up from the coil and was blown away.

'Look, Jacob, going in the water's not obligatory. No one's holding a gun to your head. Just driving around the island and having a look at Joey's places is enough.'

'I know.' But Joey's places were also Wayan's places, I thought. I sat there and thought some more about Joey and Wayan, and then Agung, with that smile on his face when he thought I was about to use Quiksilver at Medewi. 'Dad, can we go back to Medewi in the morning.' My voice sounded distant to me. 'Just for a short stop?'

'Of course. It's just down the road.'

The next morning, as we turned onto the main road, Dad said to Agung, 'Another offering and another wreath were on our doorstep this morning.'

'Yes, Tom. Also for Wayan,' Agung said, sticking his cassette in the player. Gamelan music drowned out the engine noise.

Half an hour later, at Medewi, Agung hopped up and handed me Joey's freshly waxed board, a penetrating glint in his eye. 'Wayan always say to people, Never a person who come surfing with Wayan who not learn how to surf big time. Okay, Jacob?' It was the first time he'd used my name.

I nodded, turned and headed for the water, packing death. Three surfers – fast, smooth and competition-cool – were working the waves hard before the tide dropped.

Panic time didn't set in until I was out there measuring what was building up, while at the same time trying to steer clear of the other surfers. On shore, Dad and Agung sat together, one drinking and one smoking. As the first wave neared, the others paddled out and turned quickly. Two took off on the jacking peak, while the third let it pass, waiting for the one that followed. After the second wave swept through, I stared at the last one closing in. 'For big boys,' I muttered for courage. Heart jumping in my throat, I went belly down and paddled hard. Seconds later, I felt myself lifted, but the board's nose pitched up and the wave surged past, leaving me in its wake. I sat up, relieved, and looked towards shore. Agung was in old-man-surfer pose, paddling the air and pointing to some mythical wave behind him. The message was clear. Start paddling earlier.

When the next set came through, the pattern was repeated: the others getting up in a single motion and riding effortlessly, cutting back and forth, before driving hard through the tubes and flicking out close to shore.

On the third wave, I went early and felt the familiar lift again. The wave held on. The board dipped and I picked up speed. 'Satu dua.' I was up, too stunned to move. 'Three, four, five, six…' When I looked up, the board shot out from under me and I smacked the water flat and loud before surfacing in a single stroke.

I mind-heard Rap, 'Eh, it's Jakeman, ready to walk on water.'

And I had. Well, stood on it anyway, briefly – very briefly. And while four seconds didn't merit a surf mag photo, I did get up. And the satisfaction I felt in doing that at Medewi made my skin go electric. I grabbed Quiksilver, slid back on and sat up. Agung was squatting with one arm out in clothesline pose, the other one dropped, fingers pointing to his bent knees.

Minutes later, I was back out watching the next set build. I waited for the last wave again then went early. 'Satu dua.' I was up squatting on waterbeds, arms spread like Joey's, clothes-lined like Agung's. No twisting, no back foot power, no movement at all. Just sheer concentration and the 'swish' of Quiksilver on the wave and my mental clock ticking over the joyous seconds until the wave flattened out into wash, dropping me off. I looked up. Agung's arms were swaying over his head like he'd joined a Mexican wave at the cricket. Dad clapped and shouted something I couldn't hear, before waving me in.

***

No such movement from Agung now: just him and Made sitting together quietly, staring out here. A set is banking up, and up. It's taken a while to get here, like it started on the other side of the Pacific Ocean. The first wave's not quite as big as the Clifton tsunami that day, but it's nearly as long and shapeless, and the rocks beckon if I'm tossed. I've got about two seconds to decide what to do – surf wild or get out?

I paddle out towards the rising wave, the one I've thought about and practised for since Joey's funeral, and can you believe it? Tears fill my eyes as I recall what I said to Made earlier: 'Of all the places I've planned to surf, Medewi is the most important to me.' And her reply.

I'm scared, but also exhilarated. I mumble to Joey and Dad, 'For Wayan, okay?' Then I turn and go for it. Quiksilver dips quickly, like we're on a ski run, and I'm up and snap turn left to see the wall disappear. I'm airborne, dropping, the rocks dark splotches, blurring past, before I slap down hard, stagger and stay on. The wave fills and surges. A tube forms and I'm launched into it, tucking down, dry-holed and counting, my ears filled with the wave roar and the words Joey shouted out on Mum's waterbed. And yes, after eight surf mag seconds, there is a mist rainbow, there is golden port-holed light, and I do get through, flicking out of the wave just before it collapses, exploding over the rocks.

But unlike Joey, I can't rejoice. I paddle quickly out over the wave faces, so as not to get caught inside, then I sit up and raise my eyes to the sky, trying to stop the tears. It doesn't work. I cry – not for the first time.

They're both smiling up at me when I get back in. Still trembling a little, I sit down next to Agung. 'You and Wayan sama – the same,' he says.

He wraps an arm around my shoulders and keeps it there, like Dad did at Bangli four years earlier.

***

As we pulled away from Tulamben's Bali Coral Bungalows, I cleared the snorkelling gear off the back seat, put the bag on my lap and did what Dad had asked me to – arrange enough room in it for another wreath.

Agung stopped at the junction to the main road and spoke to Dad. 'We go left, but soon two ways we can go. Short way and long way. Both go to Padangbai for surfing.'

'You're the driver, Agung. It's up to you.'

Agung stared out the windscreen in thought. 'Yesterday I use telephone in Singaraja and talk to friend at Bangli. My friend say people find Wayan… what there is. My brother bring him to our village today.'

'Is Bangli the long way or short way?'

'The long way.'

'We'll go that way, then. And once we're there, Jacob and I will get other transport…'

'No,' Agung interrupted. 'Please. Just short stop. Must finish surfing trip together. No worries. I come back to village at night.'

'All right.'

Agung turned on to the lonely road and accelerated. 'You and Jacob please come to my village, meet my family. Even if Wayan not there yet, I want you to come.'

'How do you feel about that, Jacob?'

How I felt and what I could say were poles apart. 'Yeah, fine.'

'We'd be happy to. Thanks, Agung.'

'For me to thank you,' Agung replied. He grabbed the worn cassette and shoved it into the player. Over the noisy pings, bongs and gongs of the percussion instruments, Agung said, 'One day people in my village go to big building in Denpasar in big truck and play this music and make this cassette. And so does Wayan.'

It was cooler in Bangli, under the thatched roof of the open-sided pavilion. Quiet too, inside Agung's walled compound, away from the main road. Agung and his wife were preparing tea and cakes.

'I want you to know, Jacob, how proud I am of what you've done,' Dad said to me after a while, putting his arm around my shoulders. And there wasn't a Bintang in sight.

'Thanks, Dad.' If I said anything more, I'd have had to hide my eyes.

With no one around, there was little for us to do but sit close, letting our feet dangle, and view the carved temples and shrines and Wayan's partially built cremation stand in front of us. Like the island's once strange smells, looking at things had become familiar to us: looking at things while looking for Joey the first few days; later on looking at them and thinking about the way he used to be.

Agung appeared and came over to us. 'My daughter soon bring tea and cake,' he said.

'Bagus,' Dad answered, taking his arm from around my shoulders and wincing. 'Is a kamar kecil close by?'

Agung nodded, grinning at Dad's language efforts. 'Ada, kawanku. Datanglah dengan ku. I show you.'

When they were gone, a girl with long hair flowing down her back approached carrying a tray with cakes and cups and a small metal jug on it. Her eyes stayed lowered as she placed the tray next to me. She took a couple of steps back and stood there as still and solemn as when I first saw her behind the burnt out vehicle on Jalan Legian.

'Thank you.' I didn't know what else to say to her.

Her eyes lifted. Her gaze was open, serene. An inner smile brightened her face. 'My father say you surf for Wayan.'

'Well I…I don't know…if you'd actually call it…'

She pressed her palms together. 'For me to thank you,' she said in a voice I stored away with those clasped hands, that tear and her eyes and took back with me to Tasmania.

***

Agung takes off his thongs and strolls down to the water's edge. I expect him to light up a fag. He doesn't. He just stands there looking out at the sea.

Made watches him, occupying just half her rock.

I toss more stones as another set walls up and booms down out there. Medewi decision time again. No gun to my head. My comfort, my choice. Feeling strangely calm and satisfied; as content as I think I can ever be, I go and sit next to her.

'Your father?' she asks. 'He still watch you surf in Tasmania?'

I look at Agung, a lump of grief rising in my throat, and debate how to answer that. Should I tell her about Dad's end-the-pain drinking binge a year ago, his death and the hundreds of bushies and townies who attended his funeral – 'the ferals' on one side of the chapel and in the overflow outside, 'the smart farts' on the other? And how, as we found out down there, Dad befriended people at Woodbridge: bought drinks, loaned money, fixed cars and drop-out kids' bicycles? But what good would it do if I tell her? I decide finally. She and Agung have experienced enough heartache. 'Yes,' I lie. 'He still watches me.'

'Good… My father sees Wayan surfing now.'

'I know.'

She stands and looks down at me, that same magical smile on her face. And in that moment Medewi feels like the centre of the world to me. 'Do you want to walk on the beach?' she asks.

The roller-coaster ride is rocketing skywards again. I want to say to her, Not just this beach, Made. I want to walk with you on every beach between here and Tasmania.

Joey would have.

In memory of Bali's bombing victims

Summits

Leah burst in, her eyes wide and imploring, the phone – like a relay baton – extended from her hand. 'Quick! It's your father. You've got to talk to him right now.'

Stunned, Lhotse was slow to push herself away from the computer and take the phone. 'Dad.' Wind shrieked. Something – a tent perhaps – snapped away in the background.

'Lhotse?'

'Yes.'

His voice came in low spasmodic drones. 'I love…you.'

Tears sprung to her eyes as she glanced up at her mother and realised what was happening. 'I know you do. I…' Her voice cracked before words flew out. 'I love you too, Dad, more than anything.'

'Good… Just checking.' His breathing became suddenly audible. 'Your mother…will explain.' Then there was nothing but what had to be a storm wailing like a jet plane on the other end.

'Are you there, Dad?' she shouted.

'Yes… Will you do something…for me, please?'

'Anything.' Her mother moved to the window as if Mount Everest was close and she might somehow spot him up there.

'Talk to me…about…what you did…today.'

Tears ran down her face now, but she was intent on him not knowing that. 'Mum dropped me off at school. It was just, you know, the usual sort of day.' Geez, she had moss for brains. The day – in his mind anyway – had to be one of her best ever. She condensed all the past month's good things into it. 'But I did get an A for my short story. And, Dad, I've got a role in the school play that'll be on in the hall the week before holidays start…and next Friday is Activity Day and I'm going kayaking at

Adventure Bay and…and, Dad, tomorrow night I'm going to stay over at Nicole's. Her blue heeler's just had pups.'

'How many?'

'Seven, and they're really beautiful, and Nicole's asked if we'd like to have one, and so…what do you think?'

'Good idea.'

'You're a beauty, Dad. I'll do everything for it, promise. I'll clean up after it. I'll take it for walks every day and…Dad, the line's gone bad. Dad, can you hear me? Are you there? Daaad!'

***

'It's opening up,' her mother said, staring into the distance, her breath billowing in the Himalayan cold.

Sitting on the bench, close to the abyss, they watched the emerging sun burn away the mist, exposing the craggy mountain landscape and the river valley far below. Terraced fields, studded in small mud brick houses, started down there on the river's edge and rose steeply, maybe two thousand metres, to the ridge opposite them. Beyond the ridge was more indeterminable space, before huge snow peaks, like a jagged white wall on the universe, soared up to meet the sky.

Leah pointed to the largest peak with a banner-shaped plume of cloud flying off its summit. 'Everest is there, farthest away,' she said. 'Nuptse's on its left and your mountain, Lhotse, the softer, rounded one, is just slightly right of it. It's hard to believe their base camps are still ten days walking distance from here.'

Before today, Lhotse had only seen bits of 'her' mountain in fourteen-year-old photos, its icy flanks dwarfing the small domed tents and brightly clothed climbers in her father's expedition.

A breeze stirred, tugging at the stand of prayer flags over them. There were photos of prayer flags in the album as well. Her father had explained their meaning: yellow flags for earth, red ones for fire, blue for the deep sky, white for cloud, green for water.

32

'Can you recall what we were doing while your father was climbing your mountain?' her mother asked.

'Trying to get to hospital.' It was hardly new information. On page one of their family scrapbook was a newspaper photo with an accompanying article entitled 'Bruny Island Ferry Doubles as Sea-going Maternity Ward'. Her father's plans to get back in time for her birth were thwarted by her early arrival. Other witnesses were about that day, though: ferry passengers, crew members and, of course, Gill – their inseparable island neighbour – in the back of whose van she was born, and who sent her mother a forged obstetrician's account on April Fools' Day for 'professional services rendered'.

Her father's expedition made it to Lhotse's summit, and her mother to the Royal Hobart Hospital, where friends and a Mercury journalist came to gawk and take photos. When the question of her name came up, her mother – a teacher with a love of art, literature and alliteration – thought her own summit had been reached in the circumstances of her daughter's birth. So Lhotse took the place of Daisy. And now here she was, three days and one hour up from the start of the Everest Track, seeing those father-conquered summits fully for the first time and knowing there would never be any more.

'Yes, trying to get to hospital,' her mother mimicked, a wistful smile on her face. 'But a hiccup occurred, in a manner of speaking. It was as though you'd spotted a snake in my womb, intent as you were to get out of it.'

'Sorry,' Lhotse said, as she often did whenever her mother's mind went back to that day.

Leah fixed a glassy stare on the snow peaks again.

Crows cawed. The breeze strengthened. Prayer flags flapped, releasing their messages to the gods.

A gaunt, bearded man, sitting on the end of the bench, moved closer, an arm's length away. 'It is fantastic view, yes?' he said in a heavily accented voice.

'Yes. One I'll never forget,' Lhotse answered, surprised by the man's sudden closeness and talk.

'You know where mountain Lhotse is?' he asked.

She couldn't help smiling. 'I do, yes.' Men talking mountains were nothing new to her, so there was no reason for her to feel uneasy.

He pointed to the mountain. 'I climb it two years ago. Not so easy, but Everest so beautiful from top of there. Two years before that, I climb Ama Dablam. Not so high as Lhotse, but most beautiful mountain in all Himalaya, I think.' He pointed again. 'Just in front of Nuptse. See? One that stick up like white claw scratching the sky. Seeing those mountains now make me want to cry.'

This was new. She'd never known her father, or any of his climbing friends to shed tears over mountain views. For them, climbing mountains was a source of continual joy that peaked when they came together afterwards to talk about their latest adventure over bottles of beer and wine and bowls full of steaming food. 'So are you here to climb another mountain?' Lhotse asked, hoping that talking might brighten his mood.

'This year I cannot. That is why I am sad. I work in India now and cannot get time enough off to climb the big mountains. Too much money to fly, so I ride on bus for three days from New Delhi to Jiri, then walk to here. But I tell you, I come only for this, and all the time on bus and walking is worth everything for this.' His eyes shone over at her. 'Now I must go and get my pack and go for day walk. But tomorrow I return here one last time before I leave. You will be here in morning again?'

She looked over at her nodding mother before telling him she would be.

'Maybe I see you then.' He stood up and smiled down at them. 'Thank you for listening. Not so good if excited about mountains and there is no one to talk to.' Seemingly talked out now, he turned and left.

Figures appeared from around the bend. Supply-heavy porters coughed and gag-spat, while their trekker employers shrilled at the view. Other porters – in shorts and thongs and bent double under the burden of four-metre steel beams balanced across their shoulders – rounded the bend in slow motion, calf muscles flexing, in no position to see anything but the track that always lay another few steps ahead of them.

Dawa came up from Junbesi with her baby, Pemba, strapped to her back – his rosy nose poking out between an overly large red beanie and a thick shawl wrapped around the rest of him. Sitting down next to Lhotse and smiling her greeting, Dawa lifted Pemba out and placed him on her lap, then opened her top and offered him a swollen breast.

'How old do you reckon Pemba is?' Leah said softly into her daughter's ear.

Lhotse watched the baby feed on the dark nipple for a moment before passing on her mother's question.

'Six month old,' Dawa replied, bright-faced.

'He's beautiful,' Leah said, as she had the previous day when they first saw him at the Junbesi Inn.

Dawa nodded. 'Yes.' Her gaze dropped to her child.

Leah's arm encircled Lhotse's shoulders. 'Now that we're up here amongst all these big mountains and feeding babies,' she said quietly, 'the time's right to ask you a question that's been playing on my mind for the past few months.'

'What's that, Mum?'

Rubbing her stomach and beaming a smile, Leah answered, 'What kind of big sister you think you'll be for this one?'

***

Watching. It's what he'd spent so much of his time doing since leaving hospital. Watching his girls fix their meals, and his. Watching them scurry about the house, stopping to ask if he wanted anything, or whether he was going to be 'all right' while they were out, as if he were some drooling, rocker-bound geriatric with a knee blanket that refused to stay in place. Watching Ace, the pup, chew his latest bone and sleep at his feet. Watching tree shadows shrink and lengthen and the changing patterns out on the bay. And now, with the thrill of living still tingling away inside him, watching his girls up the track staring out at the summits.

'You tired, Michael,' Mankajie continued to pester him, over his shoulder. 'You should get in.'

There was one striking difference though between here and back home in Tassie: Mankajie, in tongue-flap mode, with his basket chair strapped to his back.

'I got this far on my own, so I can well and truly get the rest of the way on my own.'

'Maybe yes, maybe no, Michael. Last part steepest.'

Michael watched Lhotse turn and look their way. Spotting them, she waved and said something to Leah, before hopping up and scampering down the track towards them.

'You haven't changed, have you? Still rock-hard stubborn,' Michael said to Mankajie, feigning annoyance.

Mankajie was also incredibly determined, tough and loyal. Traits he owed his life to. From his hospital bed, he'd told everyone how, after the blizzard ended, Mankajie and two other Sherpas spotted the top of his tent protruding from a snowdrift. How they dug down and got him out. How, for six days, Mankajie carried him down Everest and on to Lukla and the airstrip where a helicopter evacuated him to Kathmandu. Back in Tasmania two days later, he had five toes and the ends of three fingers amputated and spent three months at home recuperating before insisting on bringing Leah and Lhotse back to Kathmandu with him and taking the eleven-hour bus ride to Jiri. Mankajie met them there with that same basket chair on his back, as though he'd never taken it off. All the way up to Junbesi, Mankajie cajoled him to get in it. Only twice, on the steepest descents, did he grudgingly relent.

'For memory sake only,' he said to Mankajie, as he struggled to get in the chair.

'Memory for me too,' Mankajie answered, stooped over again under his familiar weight.

Getting in the last word had become a competition between them.

'I think the word stubborn come back with you from Australia, Michael,' Mankajie retorted, readjusting his chair straps.

'Stubbornness was here long before people like me came. At least take that great lump of a thing off your back and stow it somewhere out of my sight. It gives me nightmares just looking at it.'

Mankajie's weathered face broke into an eye-squinting smile. 'Cannot do. I think maybe Australia doctor make mistake. Take some brain off with your toes. Chair keep you happy dreaming, remember, Michael?'

'Yeah, yeah.'

Lhotse slowed. Eyes flicking from one to the other, she walked towards them measuring her father's mood.

Mankajie edged closer to Michael. 'If you not want to use chair, maybe I go find wood for fire. Use chair for that. Or maybe I carry Pemba with firewood…maybe Dawa too.' He gave Michael a last smile before greeting Lhotse warmly and going up the track to join his wife and son.

'How're you going, Dad?'

'All right, though I'm ear-sore from Mankajie telling me to get in his basket like I'm some lump of wood. We'd be at the bench now if I could've muzzled him.'

'I'm sure you've been very patient with him, though.' Her tight-lipped smile widened.

'Monk-like.'

She put a guiding arm around his waist, knowing that she was the only one who could do that, protest-free. 'Come on, Dad. There's something for you to hear that'll make the walk back to Junbesi a lot easier for you.'

'Good. We'll ensure Mankajie hears about it too.'

***

Lhotse sat her father down between her and Dawa and watched him look out at Everest for the first time in three months.

His transformation was immediate. 'No blizzards up there now intent on ripping climbers off the slopes,' he noted. 'Not so much as a cloud, just mountains shouldered in mountains, glowing in snow light… Magnificent, isn't it?'

'Uh huh.' The topic wasn't high on Lhotse's priority list now. She motioned for her mother to exchange places with her, then she sat back down and waited, watching them closely.

'Is what's out there worth the trip back?' her mother asked her father after a while.

He wrapped his arm around her. 'Absolutely.'

'So it's enough? You're not missing being up there on a summit looking out over the world again.'

'No. Nor am I missing blizzards and frostbite and lying around in the grip of death. Summits are well past their use-by dates for me.'

'Not for me.'

'What?' He scowled at her, mystified. 'You want to do some climbing?'

'No, no climbing, at least in the way you perceive it… It's just that I'm pregnant.' She paused to watch his jaw drop and his eyes swell. 'And this time I'd much prefer it if you, rather than ferry passengers and crew, were there with Lhotse to witness the birth.'

'Are you past three months?' he asked, barely breathing.

'For the second time in almost fourteen years, yes, I've managed to get that far. Well past, in fact. Six weeks past, and doing it nicely, thank you.'

He looked around, dumbfounded, before taking Leah's hands in his. 'And you took that long, hard bus ride and walked all the way up here pregnant before saying anything to me?'

'We're a climbing family. Besides, I just thought it right that we should get here first before sharing our summits.'

He stretched his arms out like a priest blessing his congregation and shouted, 'Did you hear that?' as if the others were up there on Everest instead of here on the bench. 'My wife is almost five months pregnant! You beauty!'

'We are so happy for you, Leah,' Dawa chimed in.

'It is best news, best news,' Mankajie congratulated her, thumbs up. 'I carry you back to Junbesi in chair.'

'Thank you, Mankajie, but I'll enjoy the walk.'

'Okay. But I stay close if you tired.'

'Not as close as me,' Michael piped up.

'Then you must get in basket,' Mankajie said. 'Because Leah walk too fast for you now.'

'No more basket rides, Mankajie, except for apprentice climbers Pemba's age. Leah'll slow down for me, won't you, my heart?' he coaxed, his shortened fingers stroking her blonde hair, his gaze all over her.

'Keep those tactics going,' she told him, 'and you'll never want for close, extended company.'

Lhotse felt herself squirm in embarrassment, as her mother tossed in '…of the know-what-you-like-and-how-you-like-it variety.'

'Leah, you will name your baby Everest?' Mankajie asked.

She laughed. 'As it appears my husband will be with me during its birth, I think something closer to ground level might do, like Daisy or Max, if that's okay with the baby's father and sister?'

'Fine by me, Mum,' Lhotse answered, stretching forward and eyeing her father. He was staring at the summits and didn't appear to be listening. 'Dad. Are Daisy or Max okay for the baby's name?' Lhotse repeated.

He could only nod in response, his eyes filling with tears.

Lhotse lost her smile. The image of her mother, staring out the window the day he was dying up there, filled her mind. The two of them standing horrified in her sun-struck room: and the next few days the frantic communication with Canberra, before that rapturous moment when the phone rang and his garbled voice – then Mankajie's ('Michael okay, Michael okay') – came through over his cell phone. She looked down into the abyss then back up at Everest measuring the difference. How will I go as a big sister, Mum? Lhotse said to herself, her smile returning. Just watch me.

Remembering Nurila

Rahman was wary and uncomfortable in a city without mosques and minarets, though heights didn't bother him. He refused Kien's offer of a seat and continued to pace the roof's edges, squinting at the antenna-littered skyline before lowering his eyes to the street, where motorbikes prattled past and groups of Western tourists talked and laughed over the street noise. While the men held little interest for him, the women with their free-flowing hair, breast-revealing tops and tight jeans or shorts both aroused and repulsed him. No burqas, veils, or scarves, so they held few secrets, he reminded himself. Like the produce at the open markets, what they offered was on display for all to see. Nonetheless, he continued to eye them.

'Many places to do this,' Kien said, continuing to work at the table. 'But Madame Phi Phi Club across street best, I think.'

'I see it.' Despite his English training back in Afghanistan, Rahman still felt awkward communicating in that language, especially in a place as strange as Ho Chi Minh City. He studied the club's name – beamed in red neon light – and its small windows and door, before instinctively putting a hand to his boyish beard, which, like the hair on his head and his Afghani clothes, was no longer a part of him. Besides the language and this country, there was also the lingering strangeness of adjusting to the person he'd become.

A distant plane whined and glinted in the sunlight descending into Tan Son Nhut Airport. Rahman's hands – lifted in prayer minutes earlier – lifted again as he held an imagined missile launcher against his right shoulder. As he took aim, the memory of his last day with Nurila came flooding back.

He walked up the slope and sat on a slab of rock, the spring sun warm on his back. Despite the distant crackle of gunfire and thuds of mortar shells and bombs coming from the distant mountains, he tingled with happiness. His marriage to Nurila, who he'd been allowed to choose for his wife and who loved him, was just two days away. As well, the long drought was over. The stream ran clear and fast behind him. Small birds darted past, disappearing in the lush grass. Goats fed. Poppies grew tall and deeply red, and fruit trees drooped, heavy with ripening fruit. He'd been a little boy holding on to his father's hand when he'd last seen so much colour and life in the land.

He waited and watched, and thought about Nurila. Sitting up here with him on his eighteenth birthday the previous day, she'd lowered her veil for the first time to reveal what lay beneath those alluring arched eyebrows and dark almond eyes. Her cheekbones stood out like cords of rope. Her skin was smooth, her nose perfectly straight. She took his hand and looked up at him, smiling an invitation for later. Her boldness stunned him and set his mind to calculating the exact number of hours until they were finally married.

Down in the village, people remained oblivious to the mountain fighting and the planes – glinting like daylight stars – that passed high overhead. Men riding donkey carts and bicycles moved slowly over the rutted village track, or they worked the fields, or made mud bricks for walls; while at the near end of the village women huddled around the stream, chatting and washing clothes. His mother and Nurila's were together down there and appeared to be doing all the talking.

He smiled seeing Nurila slip out her back door with pots of kabuli and tea in her hands. She glanced around to ensure no one was watching before lengthening her stride coming up the slope.

Another plane sounded. This time, though, it dropped quickly and shrieked in low. As villagers looked up in alarm, the ground lifted in a huge, roaring fireball of earth and rock, hurling him backwards as if shot by a gun. He scrambled to his feet, dazed and bleeding, and watched the plane soar back up into the heavens, leaving behind a fog of grit and destruction, demented screams and Nurila's tattered body below him. As he raced towards her, his own screaming was all he heard.

Digging frantically with spades, hoes and hands, men retrieved the dead, while women did what they could for the injured and traumatised.

Two days later, after twenty-one villagers – including his mother, Nurila and her family – were buried, Rahman left the village and headed up the valley to where the Taliban fought Westerners from outside their mountain caves.

A tooting horn and shrill laughter brought his mind back. The plane was gone. His empty hands hung at his side. Feeling utterly disconnected from life, he eyed the Madame Phi Phi Club again before turning to watch Kien. In non-Moslem countries too, he thought, Al-Qaeda's contacts were skilled, efficient and dedicated to the cause of jihad, or at least their own version of it. He took a last look at the heat-paled sky then moved over to the table. 'Western people go to that Phi Phi place?' he asked.

Kien looked up, an attentive expression on his face. 'Yes. Maybe nine or ten tonight best time for them. Always door open, always tour bus come, always line of Westerners who go in then.' He used his hands to shift his prosthetic leg so Rahman could sit next to him, then he started to explain his plan in detail, pausing long enough to point to the tape and wiring, the detonator and explosives vest strewn across the table.

Tunnelling Cu Chi

Mum and Dad offered them up as a choice: the Mekong Delta as part of a family foursome, or the Cu Chi tunnels on my own. Where's the choice? I asked myself. I'd have crawled to Cu Chi rather than do the family togetherness bit down at the Delta. Cu Chi means independence. It means Grandad. It means seeing the only place in Vietnam I'd ever heard about before arriving here four days ago. Of course, Mum and Dad have been to Cu Chi. Twice, in fact: the last time in 1993. They didn't do the tunnels, though; just attended a memorial service there and did what military families and their offspring do at such events. My world then – swings and slides, train sets and Play School television time – didn't qualify me for an airplane ticket, so I stayed at my grandmum's.

I'm still thinking about all this when the Cu Chi tourist bus rolls up. A line forms quickly and I'm slow to get in it. By the time I get inside, the bus is packed and it looks as though I'll be standing all the way to Cu Chi, until I spot a seat towards the back and head for it. The only local in the group is sitting in the window seat. I'm not sure she'll understand me. 'Is this seat taken?' I ask, slowly.

When she looks around, my solo-to-Cu Chi decision rings up another star. Her face is heart-shaped and she has bright, bird-like eyes and full, upturned lips red with lipstick. She smiles as though she's been saving the seat especially for me. 'No. No one is here,' she answers in perfect English.

I sit, grinning my thanks. She's wearing jeans and a long-sleeve Snoopy Dog T-shirt. Wishful thinking, maybe, but I reckon she's about my age, and without a doubt one of the best-looking girls I've seen in Vietnam, especially from this close.

Out of the city centre and over the Saigon River we go before market stalls, choked with people and produce, start narrowing the road. Traffic backs up. Blue exhaust thickens and rises in the air. Rusted-out buses and lorries blare their horns and rev their engines as though noise will clear the traffic jam. Armies of motorbikes converge. A few break away, darting around vehicles, peeling off and racing down side streets looking for quick escapes. I try to use what's going on out there as a conversation starter, just to test the girl's geography. 'Where I come from in Tasmania, you wouldn't see this many people in a month.'

She smiles at me politely, nothing more, before looking back out the window.

Perhaps that extra Cu Chi star isn't merited after all. I shrink back into my seat, leaving her to the view.

We clear the bottleneck finally and start zipping along again. Thirty minutes later, we turn onto a secondary road and the land turns green with coconut palms, mango trees and rice fields. We stop next to a line of open-walled stalls. Everyone but the girl piles out. We buy drinks and small cakes and gather around an old, toothless lady making traditional rice paper.

Moments later, a man wearing shorts and a conical peasant's hat rushes up to me and thrusts a camera in my face, 'Photo, photo, please.'

I backpedal, nearly tumbling into a roadside ditch. 'No, thanks. I don't want one.'

He points to a big, bulky, white-haired passenger standing with a thick snake draped around his neck like a massive horseshoe.

'The camera's mine,' the man drawls in an American accent. 'The snake's his. I've got it out on short-term rental. I thought the folks back home might appreciate the photo.'

The snake's tongue starts flicking out as its head and tail slowly encircle the man's calves.

'I don't mean to impose on ya', but I just need someone with some camera sense to look in the view finder and push a button before my knees start ta buckle.'

'Oh, right.' I trust the snake's been given a sedative. 'Yes, I can do that for you.' I take a couple of shots and hand the camera back to the snake's owner, who passes it on.

Other passengers drift closer. Money changes hands. Men snake-pose and joke while their partners click more photos. It occurs to me then that the only passenger not involved in all this is the girl. I glance up at her in the bus. It's like nothing's going on down here. She's not even watching. Instead, she's got her eyes fastened on the road with the same concentrated look as the old rice paper lady's in the stall.

Arriving at the Cu Chi tunnels' visitors' centre half an hour later, we're escorted into a large room with a display case cross-section of the tunnelling system and a large map detailing the two hundred and fifty kilometres of Viet Cong tunnels constructed in the area during the war. We sit in rows and our guide turns on an old black and white video entitled 'Nguyen – Legendary Mother and American-Killer Hero.' Not something that's likely to gain prime-time viewing at the local cinema in Hobart. It's like Nguyen has been transposed onto one of those ancient, spotty First World War film clips when trench warfare was all the go. There's Nguyen firing her rifle up in the air, then across a field before scaling an embankment to follow the bullet. There's her tending to wounded soldiers, distributing food in a village and playing with her baby; all interspersed with shots of distant explosions, battleground bodies and smoking planes plummeting to the ground. Joan of Arc in Viet Cong combat gear, I reckon. Anyway, it doesn't take long before I grow restless, along with ninety-nine per cent of the other tourists.

As I consider getting up and leaving, I spot the one per cent still video-gripped. The Vietnamese girl is sitting alone at the end of the row in front of me. I must have missed her coming in. Her head's dropped and she's dabbing away at her eyes with a handkerchief, before glancing up at the video and dabbing away some more. She, not the legendary mother and American-killer hero, keeps me in my seat.

Nguyen's adventures thankfully end soon and our guide offers to answer questions. Audience mood could make it dangerous for me to ask any, like – How many minutes did it take to make the video? So I stay quiet, as does everyone else. Our guide seems happy with that. 'Ladies and gentlemen,' he says moments later, 'it is now time to see small part of famous Cu Chi tunnels. Please follow me.' With his flip-flops slapping the floor, he leads us out.

I look back and notice the girl hasn't moved. I debate which way to go before going over to her. 'Are you okay?' I ask.

Her eyes glisten up at me. She puts on that same magnetic smile as before and the inner me swoons, silently. 'Yes. I just want to sit here a little longer,' she says. 'I'll come soon.

'I'll see you out there then.'

As the group crosses the car park, I catch up and we step onto a track that leads into rubber trees speckled in sunlight. It doesn't take long, in these surroundings, for stories of Grandad to fill my mind – one in particular.

On the far edge of the rubber plantation, our guide stops and faces us. 'Ladies and gentlemen, during war, American planes drop seventy million litres of poison on Vietnam. Forty million litres called Agent Orange. Much drops here. Agent Orange horrible because not just kill plant life, but also cause cancer, stillbirth and birth defect. From where you stand, as far as eye can see, nothing above ground after Agent Orange drop here in war…'

'Nowhere this lush in Texas,' the big American mutters next to me.

'…but ladies and gentlemen, you now see how land recover.' The guide points to his right. 'Last week I see cobra in grass.' He pauses while tourists glare at the spot like the snake might still be there. Then he takes a knife from his pocket and cuts into the trunk of a rubber tree. He collects oozing sap on his finger and holds it up in the air. 'And ladies and gentlemen, rubber here best in world for making con… con… What is word I want?' he asks, playing with his audience now.

'Condoms,' a male voice rings out, prompting titters from a few.

'Yes, those.' Like a circus master inviting his audience to view the next ring, he sweeps his left arm around towards a grassy section of dipped earth. 'And there, ladies and gentlemen, is where one huge American bomb hit. 'But does it kill anybody?'

From the middle of that crater, a circle of earth rises up out of the ground. Two hands hold it in place above a man's grinning face.

'No, ladies and gentlemen, it does not.'

The American mutters again, 'He's lookin' fresh-faced for havin' been down there the past thirty-five years.'

The man in the hole sets his earthen cover to one side and hoists himself out.

'Maybe there is damage that Viet Cong have to repair fast. But, ladies and gentlemen, there is no damage now. Who will go in and see?'

A few women nudge their men forward.

I notice the girl's still not here. When I look around, I spot her where the cobra's been. Amongst all the noise of male protests, laughter and camera instructions, I watch her move awkwardly through tree shadow, like she's just sprained an ankle or twisted a knee. She stops and takes a bunch of flowers out of her daypack, then bends down and places them against a tree trunk. She stands up straight, bows her head and presses her palms together, moving them from her forehead to her chin in prayer.

Our guide continues his commentary. 'Ladies and gentlemen, American invaders learn it take more than bombs and poison to stop freedom-loving Viet Cong from digging more tunnels to Saigon River, and under American 25th Infantry Division headquarters, and closer and closer to Ho Chi Minh City. Americans train dogs to find tunnel holes, but clever Viet Cong spread American after shave and uniforms around holes.' He inhales deeply and dramatically. 'The dogs smell and go away. The enemy also train soldiers they call "Tunnel Rats" and sometimes they find holes and go into tunnels. But booby traps kill them. Now, ladies and gentlemen, we go see those booby traps.' He leads us to a line of shallow pits. The first is the shape and size of a large bed. Rows of bamboo stakes are embedded at the bottom, pointing upwards. 'Here is example of first Viet Cong trap against American invaders,' our guide says.

Against Australians also, I think. Cameras flash and my stomach churns. The story about my grandad, told to me by Dad, takes over my mind – the gaps filled in by films, books and my imagination.

The suspect village was up ahead. A track lay metres to his left, but no way would Sam be using it. It could be mined, or booby-trapped, and if the VC were close by, they'd surely be watching it. He knelt down on one knee in a pocket of thick scrub and listened and watched. The hot air shimmered. Insects buzzed him. Birds called out. He thought he heard a monkey chattering in the distance. Nothing man-made, though. So he got out his water bottle and took a drink. And for a few moments on this, his last day as a forward scout, he allowed his mind to wander and daydream about what was ahead. Tomorrow it was tour over or, as the Yanks often said, 'Mission accomplished.' He checked his watch. In twenty-six hours and thirteen minutes, he'd be on the short timers' chopper back to Saigon. A night at Madame Phi Phi's sucking her coldest tinnies dry would prime him for the trip home, readjust his eyes to neon and headlights, his backside to bar stools, his ears to the Stones ('I can't get no...'). Then out to Tan Son Nhut Airport to board the 707 salvation express to Sydney; and from there to Hobart and Lisa and their son, Seth, and the new scrubber, Annie: until now, just a baby's chubby-cheeked face on a photograph.

Sam brought his thoughts back. It was quiet out there, like the scrub and trees and animals, and maybe the VC, were listening too. He inched forward, his nerves tingling. A clearing came into view. Just metres away, a cooking pot sat on the remains of a fire. Smoke skimmed off it. Rocks and plank board seating surrounded it. Half a dozen huts, perched on posts like giant crabs, occupied the far side of the clearing. Stick ladders led up to them, hammocks hung between them. He could almost smell the inhabitants. Sure enough, moments later two men in black pyjama uniforms came out of the trees carrying armloads of wood. When they called out, more men and a woman – automatic rifles slung across their backs – emerged from the first hut and started to descend.

Time to go. As he drew back, the scrub rustled beside him. A low growl sounded before a dog's pointed head stretched through the high grass, its fangs bared, the hair on the back of its neck rising. It growled louder, then barked. Shouts came from the clearing. Seconds later, VC started running towards him. Sam shot the dog with a single bullet, then sprang up and took aim with his M-16. A quick volley cut down two VC, but the others fanned out, finding cover. His platoon would hear. They'd know what to do. He turned and ran, veering off in the wrong direction and tripping over cutting grass. Scrambling up, bleeding, he heard the bush crackle behind him. The VC were moving too fast. He had no choice but to get on the track. Reaching it moments later, he cut left just as shots rang out, whining over him. Twenty seconds to his platoon, his frantic mind repeated, just as more shots zipped past, tearing pieces off trees. The track widened, turned leafy. Ten seconds, nine, eight… The ground collapsed, flinging him forward. In an instant, his body lay impaled on a bed of stakes, twitching, blood dripping.

'Now ladies and gentlemen, please listen carefully,' our guide calls out, bringing me back. He takes money out of his pocket and waves it in the air. 'I tell you little story. If person can answer my question after it, I give them two American dollars. One day, American soldier fall into this trap. He sit up, look around very surprised and climb out. There is not scratch on him. Why?'

A sigh escapes the American's mouth before he answers. 'Because other soldiers had fallen in before him.'

'Yes, very good. Three other Americans... Money for you.' He holds out the reward. Seeing the American glowering at him, not moving, the guide shoves the money back in his pocket and starts talking about the components of the other traps.

I see the girl hobbling along on the periphery now, listening, but not looking at the traps. The American notices her too. With each alternate step, she tilts to the right, lifts her left foot, lunges forward and stabs the foot down again. It's not just the foot, but her entire leg that's the problem. It's got to be artificial. She catches me gawking at her and smiles before looking away.

The last trap's the smallest and simplest. It's a block of wood with a small hole in the middle. Pressing the block down propels a barbed metal spike up through the hole to impale a boot.

'One spike,' our guide says, 'but each time American step on this trap, three soldiers die. Why?' He offers no money this time.

Eyes fasten on the American. But he stays quiet.

I don't. 'The soldier has a spike through his foot.' My stomach is turning over big-time. 'Two of his mates try to lift him off. Under the wooden block is an explosive device. It detonates when the block is lifted.' People's eyes are on me now, including the American's and the girl's.

'Yes, very good. There are people here today who know much about these things.' That thought stills him for a moment before he snaps back with more commentary. 'Now, ladies and gentlemen, when American tunnel rats go in tunnels, what are they thinking, and what is it like for them? For answers, come with me and you find out.'

As people move on, I find myself walking beside the American. 'Are you in Vietnam for long?' I ask him, as we round a bend.

'Long enough ta' see a few things on the ground,' he answers, 'that I missed seein' from the air last time I was here.'

What he says acts like a lure: I bite. 'Wartime, was it?'

'It was, yes. I…' He stops. 'M'name's Wes Cole, by the way.' He extends his hand.

After I shake it, giving him my name, Wes steps closer and lowers his voice. 'So, Sean, how come ya' know so much about booby traps?'

'I've read a bit about the war, the types of weapons used and that sort of thing.' I debate whether to tell him more. When he doesn't respond, I decide I will. 'And my grandfather fought here. He was a forward scout with an Australian SAS unit, and also one of the first trained tunnel rats in the war.'

'Ouch.' He takes a moment to find a more meaningful response. 'Did he survive?'

'No.'

'I'm sorry. More'n the Viet Cong and North Vietnamese suffered and died in that horrible war, as we both know.' He rubs the back of his neck. His eyes wander. 'I read somewhere once that nothin' feeds forgetfulness better than war. I 'spose that has to do with the survivors wantin' to bury the memories of what they've seen and done.'

We walk on before my curiosity gets the better of me again. 'You're a pilot, then?'

'I was.' He heaves a sigh and stops.

I stop with him. The last few tourists pass.

'Just quietly,' he says in a low, confidential voice, 'I flew one of those planes that dropped…' He pauses as if searching for the right word… 'the defoliant our guide's been talkin' about. Not that we knew back then what the effects would turn out to be.' He lifts his eyes to the sky. 'From up there, son, the world had a serene beauty to it: pure blue sky, sunlight flashin' off the C-123's wings, the green landscape slidin' by below. Closin' in on the target area, I'd take the plane down to a thousand feet, level off and signal for Chuck Henderson, the flight engineer, to play the Moody Blues through the earphones.' He glances at me. 'Ever hear of 'em?'

I shake my head.

'No, 'spose not. Long time ago.' He starts singing quietly.

'Nights in white satin, never reaching the end,
Letters I've written, never meaning to send.
Beauty I'd always missed, with these eyes before.
Just what the truth is, I can't say any more.'

After a small smile pause, Wes continues, 'Over the drop zone I'd check the wing ducts were open before turnin' the defoliant release valve on, and for the next three minutes our cargo sprayed out, trailin' the wings in long, wavy banners, before fadin' and driftin' down.' He drops his head again and gives a little smile, like maybe he feels he's said too much. 'Anyway, my wife's been after me for years ta come back over here. Somethin' about purgin' grief and arrivin' at some sort of resolution.' His eyes meet mine. 'Ya know much about that?'

I feel complimented. His confiding openness makes me feel older than I am. 'I've heard people talk about it.'

'I can tell ya, son, the difference between talkin' about it and doin' it is considerable.'

We move on and minutes later arrive at a large pit with four earthen steps leading steeply down to the start of a tunnel tucked away in one corner.

The guide calls out, 'Ladies and gentlemen, welcome to small part of Cu Chi tunnels. Below this ground are two sections for tourists to go through. Small lights are on floor so you see where you go. Tunnels are one-metre high, eighty centimetres wide. For people who not want to go in tunnels, there is American M-48 tank that Viet Cong destroy with landmine up the track. It is where we all meet in fifteen minutes.' He does another sweeping arm movement, inviting people into the tunnel.

No one moves immediately. People look around to see who'll volunteer to go in first. Finally, two couples descend, get down on all fours and scuttle into the tunnel. A few more follow. Another minute passes before Wes sets off for the pit – perhaps forgetting he's got his daypack on – and descends. Surprisingly, the Vietnamese girl hobbles over to the steps after him. She presses her hands against the pit wall and descends too – one crab-like step at a time. No way am I not going to follow her. I head down.

Even on his hands and knees, Wes has to lower his head to clear the opening. No sooner is he in than the Vietnamese girl drops down and, dragging her artificial leg behind her, disappears inside. I follow.

On our left, Christmas-size red and yellow lights line the dun-coloured floor. But Wes is like a third wall blocking what's up ahead. A few metres in, the girl's leg starts to squeak.

'Anybody back there?' Wes asks, having to know there was.

'Yes,' the girl and I answer together.

'That squeakin' noise isn't the floor protestin', is it?

The girl tells him what it is. 'I forgot to oil it before coming in,' she adds.

Both Wes and I laugh, appreciating her ability to joke about herself.

'That's a comfort, anyway,' Wes says. 'That it isn't the floor squeakin', I mean.'

We crawl on, the tunnel sweating moisture, and after a while Wes's daypack starts scraping the tunnel. 'I'm sweatin' a river in here,' he admits. 'I brought along a water bottle, but it might as well be sittin' on the dinin' room table back home for all the good it's doin' me… Oh m'golly. Ya might wanna' slow down roundin' this here bend.' He stops, and there's just the sound of his heavy breathing before he asks the girl, 'Does that leg of yours protest more when it's goin' forwards or backwards?'

'I don't know. It's only ever gone one way – forward.'

'It's just that…'

'For me there is plenty of room in this tunnel. I would be happy to carry your pack.'

'That's good of ya, but unless this here tunnel has a sudden growth spurt, I won't be pullin' it off me any time soon.'

'How much do you value its straps?'

'A whole lot less than I value gettin' round this bend.'

'I have some small scissors,' she says, taking her own daypack off. 'I think I can cut your pack off and put it in mine.'

'I'd be grateful.' Finding the scissors, the girl moves up to him. Settling her upper body along his back, she begins snipping away at the right strap.

'I'm thinkin' introductions are in order. I'm Wes Cole and I'm pleased you're in here with me.'

'I'm Tien Nhu, Mr Cole.'

'Call me Wes.'

'And I'm Sean,' I add.

Moments later, the strap's cut through. A spray of dirt falls as Tien pulls the daypack off his back, and we all eye the roof anxiously before Tien gets out the water bottle and passes it up to Wes.

Wes has a drink and thanks her, returning the bottle. Taking in a deep breath, he wriggles around the bend saying, 'I doubt m'coffin'll be any tighter than this.'

'My father once told my grandmother, Mr Wes, that when he suffered from claustrophobia in here, he formed an image of my mother waiting for him in the next chamber. She was wearing her ao dai pant suit and holding up a cup of rice wine mixed with snake's blood and gall bladder in one hand, and a bowl of steamed rice dumplings in the other.'

'Was your father headin' for her, or tryin' ta get away from her?'

Tien's laugh is quick and high-pitched. 'Heading for her, Mr Wes.'

'We move ta different dietary tunes, your father and me… So he's been down here before, then?'

'Yes.'

'And your mother too?' I ask, my curiosity taking hold again.

'Only in my father's imagination.'

'Come in, Wanda,' Wes says, 'in your bright red miniskirt, low-cut ruffled blouse, high heels and black lace stockin's, grinnin' that grin and holdin' up a bottle a Lone Star beer in one hand and a plate a steak, grits and black-eyed peas in the other.'

'Wanda's your wife, Mr Wes?'

'She is.'

'And are those thoughts working for you now?'

'I believe they are, yes. Oh m'golly.' Dipping his knees and rolling his shoulders, he scrapes around another bend before stopping. 'Your father's got one colourful imagination. That wine concoction has yet ta take off big where I come from.'

'Perhaps no one feels the need for an aphrodisiac where you come from.'

'Ah… Well… That's somethin' I wouldn't know a whole lot about.' He chuckles politely and starts to crawl on when suddenly the lights go out. 'Now I know what it's like livin' in an ink bottle,' Wes responds quickly. 'I'd be prepared ta take up smokin' if anyone's got a cigarette and a lighter.'

'The lights are out!' I shout, the words echoing up and down the tunnel. 'We can't see down here!'

Just the echoing, that stops. A cold fear spreads to my chest and throat.

'The lights are out!' Wes shouts next.

Just the echoing, then nothing.

Time passes listening hard before Tien gives a little laugh, meant, I'm sure, to balance what we're feeling. 'We know where there is light, don't we,' she says. 'So I think now is the time to teach my leg something new. Can you crawl backwards now, Sean.'

'Yes.' I do, my feet feeling their way back for a few seconds, before I stop.

Her straining voice joins the sound of her protesting leg as she struggles backwards, before jamming that leg into the wall. She repositions herself and moves on. Wes follows. Guided by Tien's sounds, I crawl back some more before letting her catch up.

'You might wanna' warn your father ta check the lights before he comes back down here again,' Wes says when Tien stops to rest.

'My father is dead, Mr Wes.' Her voice quickens. 'But I will surely tell my relatives what has happened here.'

'Including your mother?' I ask.

'She is dead too… Okay, I'm ready to go again.'

'Before you do,' I interrupt, trying to keep up with everything she's saying, 'I've got an idea. If I hold your leg and guide it towards me, it might make things easier for you.'

'Have we known each other long enough for you to do that?'

I don't know whether to laugh or apologise. One thing's certain, though. Like Wes, I'm really happy she's down here with us.

Tien chuckles and answers her own question. 'Yes, I think I have known you long enough. Thank you, Sean.'

And so we move backwards together, and rest and talk and move on some more.

At one stop, Tien says, 'Now we can understand what it was like for people to be underground when the planes went over, can't we? My grandmother told me stories about her village at such times. About how, once the air went still again, the villagers would come out of their bunkers brushing the dirt off their heads and shoulders and frowning at a strange orange mist that swept in on the breeze. About how the village elder, pressed to answer everyone's questions, could only maintain a dignified calm and admit he'd never seen such a mist before. About how the mist stayed for hours obscuring trees and fields, settling into the stream and on the crops, sticking to ox carts and bicycles, seeping through cracks in thatch walls and badly fitting doors. Because it smelled sweet, and no one collapsed or died, the village elder thought the mist was harmless. And so the villagers went on with their chores, as they always had, while the chemicals worked silently away inside them.'

Her voice pauses and there's just the black silence for maybe a half minute before she starts talking again. 'Planes continued to fly low over her village, filling the air with orange mist. Plants and trees started to shrink and die. One day, a baby girl was born with blistered skin, tiny flippers for arms and legs and an eye where her right cheek should have been. After incense sticks were lit and the spirits of ancestors consulted, the village elder took the baby away and killed and cremated it over cracked, barren ground... Not nice,' she says in a light voice, as the greatest understatement of the century.

'No,' I say.

Wes stays quiet. And I think how Tien's story must be affecting him.

'I don't mean ta impose, Tien,' Wes speaks up during the next stop, 'and please tell me ta mind my own business if you feel that's not what I'm doin', but I can't help wonderin' how your parents died.'

'Cancer, Mr Wes.'

'I'm sorry.'

'A light,' Tien says quietly, moments later.

I twist my head around in every direction before I see it, bobbing like a firefly behind us. It's got to be a torch with someone on the other end of it. 'We're here!' I shout.

'We get you out,' comes the reply.

Then it's just that light bobbing and growing until it shines bright, making our eyes squint and highlighting our dirty, relieved faces.

'Problem with electricity. You last to come out,' the voice behind the light says. 'Follow me. Maybe five minute, then out.'

When the tunnel starts turning lighter shades of grey, we recognise our guide as our rescuer. Around the last bend, dusty daylight beams through. We back out of the entry into the pit, exhausted. Still on our knees, I grab Wes's hand and give it a vigorous shake. Tien extends her hand too. Blow that, I think. I wrap my arms around her, and after I free her, it's Wes's turn. With his eyes beaming with gratitude, he hugs her like a bear would a rabbit. Tien nearly disappears in his arms. Moments later, flushed and looking embarrassed, she returns his backpack.

The rest of the tour hasn't really got us. We clean up and stay together, with Wes and me walking as slowly as it takes for Tien to keep up. Back in the bus, people reclaim their same seats. So Wes sits at the front again. On the road, it's soon obvious the driver doesn't get paid by the hour: there are no stops, and it's a swerving, horn-blaring, speedway ride back to the city. Tien and I don't talk much. Conversation was much easier in the tunnel.

When we're dropped off, Wes comes up and asks if we're doing anything. I've got an hour or so to spare before Mum and Dad return, and Tien says she's got some free time too, so Wes suggests we get a bite to eat – his 'treat', he insists. As there's no shortage of eating spots, Wes quickly finds what he's looking for and we take a table at the back. It doesn't take long for us to rely on Tien again, this time for a menu translation. Once that's done and we've ordered, conversation slows.

Young girls come in every few minutes holding runny-nosed babies. They come up to our table and look appraisingly at each one of us, before extending their cupped hands Wes's way. He gives them money.

After ordering a second beer, Wes looks over at Tien. 'Ya know, I can't help thinkin' about our conversation in the tunnel today, and ya talkin' about your parents.' He pauses, perhaps not knowing where to go with his next sentence.

Tien smiles. 'And you, Mr Wes, talking about your wife.'

'Only in trusted company,' he jokes. 'It wouldn't do me a whole lotta good at home if what I said in there became universal knowledge.'

'No chance of that.'

'No. We'll soon be goin' our separate ways, won't we? Back ta who and what we know best.'

'And for you, where is that?' Tien asks.

'Ya know much about the United States of America?'

'Brad Pitt, Sunset Strip, Statue of Liberty, George W. Bush.'

He laughs. 'All important ingredients, true. Include the state of Texas in all of that and you've just about got the entire recipe.'

'And what do you do there?'

Wes lost his smile. He glanced around the restaurant, perhaps looking for more beggars to intervene. 'I'm retired,' he says finally. 'Mind if I ask ya the same question?'

'I'm a student in Australia. My parents went there seven years after the Amer…the Vietnam War ended. I was born there. I'm in Vietnam for three weeks now to visit my grandparents in Vinh Long province…and to look around a bit.'

'Well, I'm mighty pleased you are.'

I get my chance. 'So whereabouts in Australia do you live?' I ask her.

'Do you know Cabramatta?'

'Between the Opera House and the Blue Mountains, western suburbs of Sydney, train lines and freeways, and the country's best Vietnamese restaurants.'

'All important ingredients,' she says, smiling briefly over at Wes, who's enjoying the mimicry. 'Add my aunt and uncle and five cousins and you just about have the entire recipe.'

Our meals come. We eat and I give everyone a loud 'Mmmm', just to let them know I like the food, whatever it is. Wes nods getting stuck into it. Tien smiles.

'Did your parents live in Cu Chi, Tien?' Wes asks after a while.

Eating stops.

Tien takes a moment to answer. 'My father and mother fought with the Viet Cong during the American War, Mr Wes. For a long time, they lived in and around the Cu Chi tunnels…' She looks down at her artificial leg, then places her left arm on the table and carefully lifts her sleeve, exposing a forearm full of round, pale scars, like the remains of blisters. She eyes us in turn before going on… 'and my parents were exposed to the Agent Orange dropped there.' She lowers her sleeve and goes quiet for a moment. 'Anyway, after the war, those who fought against the South Vietnamese government forces and the Americans thought life would become a paradise on earth for workers. It didn't. Things were very bad here and my mother experienced two stillbirths. So my parents were prepared to go anywhere, by any type of transport, for a new start – even to the land of a former enemy. They joined seventy others on a fishing boat and, after a long, very bad trip, they got to Australia, and were allowed to stay. That wouldn't have happened if they hadn't paid for false papers and lied convincingly about which side they fought for in the war… War's horrible. But you know, each war ends and things change. Memories fade and the world keeps turning, and people who were once enemies eventually become neighbours, business partners and friends. Vietnamese, Cambodians and Thais have fought many wars in the past. Now they live peacefully and happily beside each other.'

While Wes stares at the table, my mind wanders, overrun with images of Cu Chi, of Wes's plane dropping Agent Orange from above and of Grandad and Tien's parents as enemies on the ground, trying to kill each other.

'So, Mr Wes, have you come to Vietnam as a tourist, or do you know people here?'

He looks straight at me. There's a message in his eyes, and I'm reading it.

'I'm here as a tourist,' he says. 'Though in future I think I'll be restrictin' my sightseein' activities ta places above ground.'

Tien laughs. 'Me too.' She looks over at me. 'And you, Sean?' she asks, maybe to bring me back into the conversation.

'Yeah, just a tourist. Mum and Dad are down at the Mekong Delta for the day. They gave me a choice and I chose Cu Chi.'

'I'm pleased you did.' Her eyes briefly penetrate.

'Yeah… Me too,' I say.

We finish our meals.

Playing a different person, Wes stands and makes a performance of looking at his watch. 'As I'm doing the city's nightlights' tour tonight, which ends at the club next door, I'd better go and scrape the tunnel dust off me. I want ta thank ya both. It's been a day I won't be forgettin' any time soon.' He offers his hand and Tien and I shake it in turns, thanking him. Wes hesitates, as if he wants to say something more, but decides against it and turns and leaves, paying the bill on the way out.

Minutes later, Tien and I walk out on the dimming footpath. A taxi horn toots. A peal of laughter rings out from a group of tourists nearby. The tops of buildings are catching the day's last sunlight. From one of them a dark-skinned man peers down on the street before disappearing.

Next door's flashing red neon reads 'Madame Phi Phi Club'. I've seen it before. Tien and I talk. She's got a bus to catch to Vinh Long. I've got a hotel room to go to.

As I'm stoking up the courage to ask her for an address or phone number, she says, 'So do you think Mr Wes is really just here as a tourist, Sean?'

I heard someone say once, when you're stumped for an answer, ask a question. 'Don't you?'

She shakes her head slowly and scans my face like she's trying to read something in it, or maybe not. Maybe I'm just getting paranoid. She glances at passers-by for a moment before looking at me again. 'Today has been my most important day in Vietnam,' she says, changing the topic. 'Thank you for sharing it with me.'

My heartbeat accelerates. I can feel it in my groin and temples. I nod and shake her extended hand, not wanting to let it go. After I do, she turns and heads off. 'Tien Nhu from Cabramatta,' I mutter, watching her roll and lunge down the footpath. I feel like running after her. I shout out, 'Tien, I'll see you in Australia, okay?'

She turns and puts on her best smile again. That's what started all this. It's her turn to nod now, and she says, 'Okay.' Or at least I think she does. There's so much noise on the street. I watch her continue on until she rounds a corner, waves and disappears.

I watch the people and traffic and start to feel lonely. So how do I go about seeing her again in Australia? Consult a phone book? How many people with the name Nhu live in Cabramatta? Lots, surely. Forget the phone book. There's my Uncle John in Strathfield. I'll visit him and take the train out to Cabramatta one day. Tien Nhu, around sixteen, artificial leg, second generation Agent Orange victim. That should narrow it down.

Four young Westerners round the corner Tien has just turned down. They're bantering, laughing and shoving each other, and the bloke in the lead is hobbling, exactly like Tien. By the time they pass me, they're uproarious and all four are hobbling, making a competition of it. Watching them go in the Madame Phi Phi Club, I think what stone-brain bastards they are.

I start walking towards the hotel. A passenger plane roars overhead. Across the road, a line of beggars sit cross-legged appealing to passing tourists for money. Hurrying on, I begin to think how I've never visited my Uncle John in Strathfield before. We don't really know each other. And Cabramatta's a long way to go. Maybe I should just try my luck with a phone book.

A girl holding a scrawny baby rushes up and thrusts the baby in my face. 'Money for food,' she exclaims.

I draw back, startled. It's more a demand than a request. I skirt around her and quicken my pace, losing her by weaving through the thick traffic.

Shadows and pockets of darkness are spreading. My thoughts turn to Tien again: beautiful face, a brain the size of a planet, fantastic smile; also one leg, blister-scarred skin, a future cancer ward certainty. Not that that puts me off, but…well, connecting with her back in Australia won't be the same. Cut off from the rest of the world, our lives came together today, briefly. But, as she said in the café, things change, memories fade, while the world keeps on turning. Besides, she's probably got a boyfriend – Vietnamese, most likely – or at least someone who knows what to do with that leg when feelings get warm and close. Me going up there would just complicate things for her.

I regret now having made such a fuss about seeing her again when she was leaving. I mean, we can keep in touch. I can write her a letter sometime, care of the local high school, or maybe a Christmas card. Yeah, that's it; store the memory and move on. That decided, a sense of relief spreads through me as the brightly lit Rex Hotel comes into view. Mum and Dad will want to know all about the tour, so I start working out what I'll tell them and what I won't.

Another Door

Ella's pulse beat hard and little tremors of fear shivered through her. She knew it, of course she did. She'd already passed the written part. But now, every time she closed her Learners' Handbook, her mind went blank, like road rules clicked on Alzheimers in the sponge she called her brain. Geez, she couldn't fail the driving test. Not after all the time she'd spent practising. It would take at least another month before she could do it again. That meant another month of grovelling to her parent-magnets for rides in and out of town, and having to listen to their insistent patter that 'It makes no difference at all, Ella, what time of the night it is, just ring and we'll be there to pick you up.'

Yeah, right.

Passing this driving test was all that stood between her and total independence. She had a car. For surviving her eleven DRIVE PERFECT lessons without adding to the state's road statistics, her grandparents bought it for her, compliments of their special granddaughter bank account. It was a little dream machine – eye-catching red, CD player, great speakers, quick-start engine and new retreads. Not that her parents – chorusing their little ditties to her, then going all goggle-eyed whenever she made the slightest mistake L-plating around with them – seemed to appreciate the car's features. And that was one more reason why she couldn't fail. Another month of them quaking away in their co-driver seats could well bring on heart attacks. She'd have to keep a resuscitator in the back seat and continue to play her CDs so low they could hear ants breathing along the roadside.

No. That P-plate – her plaque to parent-free driving – had to come today. She just needed to stay calm and do what she'd memorised and rehearsed these past few months. She lowered her eyes and continued reviewing. 'Always give way to the right at traffic circles… Forty kilometres through school zones… Fifty kilometres in town if not otherwise posted…' Yeah, yeah, yeah. She'd been all through this on paper. She looked up and watched an old man, shaped like a white-haired pear, enter the building and shuffle across to the woman at the counter. 'Mornin', Judy,' she heard him say.

'Good morning, Stan. Lovely to see you. That time of the year again, is it? How're those magnificent roses of yours getting on?'

'I'm fine, Judy, and m'roses are too. Got more colour in m'garden now than an artist's got on his palette. The Botanical Garden's a desert by comparison. Once I get my licence fixed up here, I might just drive over to Hertz, negotiate a leasing contract on a van and start runnin' tourists up to my place… I'll start with you. Fancy a ride up, a cuppa tea and a tour of the garden again this year?'

'Of course I would. Still driving the Morris?'

'Still am. She ticked over five hundred thousand a few weeks back, so I gave her a scrub-up and a full service to celebrate. She's outlasted Sarah, bless her magnificent soul, and m'last three dogs. My only regret is there's not enough room in the house for her.'

Judy chuckled and pointed in Ella's direction. 'I'm running a bit late, so if you want to take a seat over there for a few minutes, I'll get the paperwork organised and be with you shortly. Want a cuppa while you wait?'

'Love one, thanks.'

'If you're turning right, you must give way to any traffic approaching from the right; any oncoming traffic that is going straight ahead or turning left; and…'

The old man came over, aimed his backside over the bench and plopped down with a sigh. 'First time, is it?' he asked, directing his veined, watery gaze her way.

She closed the handbook. 'Yes.'

'It was for me too sixty-eight years ago. Been gettin' a lotta practice at it these past five years, though. After ya crank over eighty, it becomes an annual event.'

Judy approached, smiling, and handed Stan a mug of tea.

'Thank you, pet,' he said. He sampled his drink and chewed his gums before looking over at Ella again. 'But there're advantages to that. Judy's always the one who comes with me. She loves her roses, just like m'wife used to, so I look forward to her visitin'. If the truth be told, I wouldn't mind if licence renewal became a weekly event rather than a yearly one… Might have to write a letter to the newspaper about that.' His laugh was like a cough.

A thin, well-dressed man wearing glasses and carrying a clipboard came over and greeted Stan, before turning to her. 'Ella Taylor?'

Her nerve eruption was instant. She got to her feet. 'Yes.'

'I'm John Turner, your driving test assessor. Ready to go?'

She nodded to save her voice from cracking and looked back down at Stan as if she were about to start a prison sentence. 'It was nice talking to you.'

His smile deepened his wrinkles. He gave her the double thumbs up like some eighteen-year-old. 'Don't worry. You'll be right.'

He was the only one who thought so.

***

'Check the side mirror, check the back windscreen… All clear, into gear… Clutch out slowly, accelerate slowly… Be deft before turning left… Roundabouts, beware of louts… Check right before taking flight… Changing lanes, indicator reigns… Lights are red, handbrake ahead…'

Before today, she had practised three times getting out of the car park. But this time, though her memory-linked ears were perfectly tuned to her parents' instructions, the messages just weren't getting through to the rest of her. Five minutes into her driving test and she wondered what sort of ditties her parents could think up for 'stall', 'whiplash', 'near miss' and 'straddling the white line'.

She figured she'd already gone through her quota of ten stuff-up points, so what was the point in going on? She might as well find somewhere blind-man-easy to park her dream machine, with its nightmare driver, and hand over the keys (she'd probably hit the kerb, roll onto the footpath and knock over a power pole).

John Turner looked over and said, 'You've had driving lessons, haven't you?'

Embarrassment sided with despair. Yeah, at Dodge-em Cars whenever Sideshow Alley's back in town, she thought to say. Fortunately, they were stopped at an intersection ('Lights are red, handbrake ahead') and she'd just done something right.

She nodded before words spilled out. 'I've never ever driven this badly before, not even during my very first lesson.'

'I believe you. You're a potentially excellent driver who's just suffering from what I call First Driving Test Trauma Disorder. I've had many promising drivers like you who feel they want to give up at about this stage.'

The light turned green. ('Clutch out slowly…' Yeah, yeah).

'That's exactly how I'm feeling now. So do I have any more points left to lose?'

'Yes. And if I were a betting man, I'd wager you'll be a licensed driver in another half an hour's time. Just relax, concentrate and prove me right.'

***

She reckoned it all hinged on how good his eyesight was during her second attempt at parallel parking. With his glasses off and his head pulled back, it might have appeared that she'd just managed to sneak the tyres onto the concrete strip next to the kerb, or maybe not. It was that close. While other assessors and drivers drove in and out of spaces next to them, she waited, expecting the worst, and picturing herself lining up to make another driving test booking.

John Turner looked up from his clipboard. He eyed her with a smile she couldn't read and proceeded to review her mistakes, including nearly wiping them out on the first roundabout. 'But once you settled,' he went on, 'you drove well. The mistakes you made you won't make again once you're driving regularly.'

Her spirits lifted. A different picture formed before she suppressed it.

'I'll just have to add all this up to see when that might happen.'

She could hear those ants breathing now.

'Right. It looks as though that second parallel park won the bet for us.' His smile got personal. 'You've got one point to take back home with you. Congratulations.'

Her heart rocketed. Her body glowed and tingled. She felt like throwing her arms around him and screaming, 'Thank you, thank you, thank you.' Instead, she thanked him once, breathlessly, her eyes meaningfully fastened on his, though she wondered if he realised that, before she pulled out her mobile. First Leah, then Alice, then Jess… No, first her mum and dad, then her grandparents.

'Anyway, when you're finished, I'll see you inside.' John Turner, the driving God of her idolatry, got out. 'It won't take long to issue you with your P plates and licence.'

Dialling her mobile, she started composing, then gave up when her father answered. 'Dad. I got it. Because I've got the most awesome parents in the world for driving instructors, I got it. I got it, Dad! I got it!'

'Ella, that's fantastic.' No more ditties. 'We need to celebrate. Why don't we meet you at the Siam Garden for a meal? Invite your friends along – our shout. And don't worry, your mother and I'll leave early. *The Bill*'s on tonight.'

'Can Grandad and Grandmum come too?'

'Of course. We'll swing around and pick them up. Your mother's here clawing me for the phone. I'll put her on and you two can work out the details.'

***

At first, she thought Stan had fallen asleep, sitting there on the bench with his head slumped over, arms folded, his glasses on his lap. But when she sat down next to him, he raised his head and gave her a glazed look, like that of an old turtle's. He was a different man now. Something had happened.

'Tell me how ya went,' he said anyway.

'I got it.'

'Good, good. So another door opens, eh, love?'

She nodded and waited for him to say more.

He didn't.

Judy came over and sat down beside him. 'How're you getting along?'

'Fine, fine.'

'I've rung up the RACT. They'll have a tow truck here in a few minutes. After that, we'll have to think about getting you home. How about if I ring you a taxi?'

'No, don't bother, Judy. It's time I started getting used to buses.'

'Then I'll go and check the schedule. Buses to Risdon Vale stop just outside.'

'I live out near Richmond,' Ella said after Judy had gone. 'I go past Risdon Vale. I'd be happy to give you a ride.'

***

Cold Creek Road was aptly named. No sooner had they turned off on it and descended the dirt surface than the sun ducked in behind a ridge and the temperature dropped.

After they rounded a big gum tree, Stan pointed to a small weatherboard house just off the road. It was surrounded by low, lattice fencing and a colour bonanza of flowers, shrubs and small native trees. 'That's it, the governor's mansion,' he said in a flat voice.

She stopped next to the gate, took the car out of gear and lifted the handbrake. ('Out of gear, lift without fear.' Incredible. They were still there in her head.) At the front of the house was a treated-pine deck, its roof-length beams entwined in red and white geraniums. A round, wrought-iron table and two chairs occupied the feature spot beside the door, and she could make out a china teapot and cups and saucers on it, the type her grandparents always used. 'Lovely spot.'

'It suits. I want to thank you for the ride and say how much I've enjoyed talking to you.'

As well as being taught how to pour and sip tea like the Queen, she'd also learned her oldies' talk at her grandparents' place. 'It was my pleasure.' She flashed a good-time smile to balance his sad-time one. 'You're my first P-plate passenger, and a very brave one too, especially after your accident. My self-confidence has gone up a big notch with you sitting there.'

'I'm pleased to hear that… Well, goodbye.' Stan opened his door to get out.

She glanced at the house and the table and the tea set arranged for his annual visitor. Her choice. She could keep quiet and let him go, or she could ask him something timely and meaningful. 'Where are your roses?'

'At the side of the house,' he said with one leg out the door. 'You can't quite see them from this angle.'

'My mum has roses.'

His smile got real again. 'Has she? What sort?'

Ella blushed and grinned. 'The red and pink and white sort.'

'I've got those sorts too, plenty of them.'

'Do you?' Her girlfriends could wait. There were two things she was intent on doing here first, despite the cold. 'I'd love to see them.'

Sandy Heads

Jassim's first day at Brighton Primary School was his worst day ever because he'd never been separated from his mother before. After that terrible first day finally ended and he raced home to her, the sight of his father's taxi in the driveway only added to his discomfort and confusion. His father never came home during the day.

As Jassim stood there dumbstruck on the footpath – eyes tracking the paving stones leading to the back door – his father came out of the front one and called him in.

Inside, Jassim sat down at the kitchen table.

Sitting opposite, his father folded his hands and gazed down his beard at him. 'How was school?' he asked in Arabic.

'Good, Father.'

'I'm pleased.' He didn't sound it. 'Now that you've started school, you need to know what will be expected of you each night. Before your last prayers, you are to read the Koran, your schoolbooks and something from the newspaper for at least an hour. After that, you can spend one hour watching television, preferably the news.'

Prescribed reading time went up ten minutes each year after that, though television time and, later, Internet time, remained the same.

However, as Jassim's father often drove his taxi up to eighteen hours a day, it was left to his mother to oversee the instructions. She'd stand behind his father, eyes lowered, nodding, when he announced the new school year's rules. But when he wasn't there, she'd loosen her headscarf, put their Arabic–English dictionary, paper and coloured pencils on her lap and read the comics from the newspaper. She'd encourage Jassim to draw his own English cartoon characters, like The Wizard of Baghdad Id ('My house is so small.' 'How small is it?' 'Our tea towel is our carpet.')

and help him with his schoolwork. Later, she would reward him by losing track of the evening's entertainment time.

'Oh, Jassim,' she'd exclaim, feigning surprise when she caught him still on the computer, or watching something he shouldn't. After Neighbours, Wheel of Fortune, Vets to the Rescue and The Simpsons had finished for the night, she would say, 'Is it really so late? Well, just for tonight we'll skip maths and read one more story before your prayers.'

Jassim cherished this time of the evening when they learned to read and write English together.

One afternoon, during Jassim's grade six year, his father came home early. Fortunately it was before the start of Neighbours. He sat his children down in front of him and declared, 'You are not to read the newspaper or watch news on the television unless I am here with you. Is that understood?'

At school, Jassim had been taught to ask questions if he didn't understand something. 'Why, Father?' he asked, automatically raising his hand.

'The fact I've said so is enough,' he answered sternly. 'Now, while I eat, you three are to go into your rooms and do your homework. Jassim, I'll come to your room shortly to read something from the Koran and test you on it.'

An hour later, his father sat down on the edge of Jassim's bed. He placed the Koran on his lap and began quizzing his son. 'There is no God but Allah, and Muhammed is his what?'

'Prophet, Father.'

'Yes, or messenger. What is the meaning of Islam, Jassim?'

'Doing what Allah wants you to.'

'Use the words "surrender" or "submission" to the will of Allah. Now, in the eyes of Allah, all men are what?'

Jassim felt his stomach clench. There was a time when he knew all the proper Arabic words, but English had got in the way. 'Uh… All the same.'

'"Equal" is the word used in the Koran, Jassim! And what else?'

Jassim's shoulders drooped, and his eyes dropped. 'I can't remember,' he muttered.

'Brothers.' His father breathed a heavy sigh. 'What's a hadith, Jassim?'

'A trip Moslems must take once in their lifetime to Mohammed's birthplace in Mecca.'

His father's eyes closed in frustration. 'That's a hajj. A hadith is a story taken from Mohammed's life. Every hadith carries a lesson. They are used to guide believers. Remember that. Now I'm going to read you a hadith I've read to you before. After I'm finished, you're to tell me what the hadith's lesson is. He opened up the Koran to a marked page and read, "Said Muhammed to his followers, 'While a man was walking on the road, his thirst grew strong and he found a well and descended into it and drank. When he left he saw a dog hanging out its tongue and licking the ground from thirst. The man said, 'This dog's thirst is like the thirst I had,' and he went into the well again, filled his shoe with water and gave the dog a drink. And God approved of his act, and pardoned his sins.'" He looked over at his son. 'Why did Allah, our God, do that, Jassim?'

'Because... Because dogs are as important as people.'

'More than that. There is a reward for not only helping dogs, but every living creature. Remember that.' He sighed. 'All right, that'll be enough from the Koran tonight.' He pointed to the hadith he'd just read. 'By tomorrow night, you are to know this hadith well enough to recite it to me. Okay?'

'Yes, Father. You'll be coming home early again tomorrow?'

'I hope to.' He closed the Koran and stood up. 'Time for you to pray now. Goodnight, Jassim.'

'Goodnight, Father.'

***

'Well done, Jassim,' his mother said the next evening. She set the Koran on the kitchen table. 'I will tell your father you were almost...no, that you were word perfect. Now, for doing so well...'

'Mama,' Jassim blurted out. 'Will there be a war in Iraq?'

'Who's to say. Now...'

Again he interrupted, 'America, England and...Australia.'

'How do you know this?'

'It's impossible not to know. At school, students ask me if I'm going back home to fight Australians in the war, and in class Ms Roberts talks about it because students ask her about it. When I go to the library, there are newspapers there, and I can't help seeing what's on the front page. There are men in suits and Saddam Hussein and soldiers with guns and airplanes and ships and rockets and tanks…and there's huge writing that…that sometimes makes you think people here like war.'

Jassim's mother glanced over at his sisters watching television, before meeting his eyes again. 'Has anyone been bad to you at school?' she asked in a low voice.

'No, not really. There's just a bit of stirring, that's all.'

'What means this "stirring"?'

He reverted to Arabic. 'It's like teasing. Boys I'm playing soccer against sometimes do it after I score a goal against them, or sometimes it happens after the teacher praises me for something. It's nothing serious.'

'You will tell me if something serious happens, won't you?'

'It won't.'

She searched his face for a moment. 'Tell me, Jassim, are there ever discussions about Iraq in your class?'

'Sometimes. But I just listen, Mama.'

'Good. Don't do anything more than that. You must not say anything about Iraq to anyone at school.'

'Mama, when the war starts, will we be told to leave Tasmania?'

'I don't think that will happen, no. People here have been very good to us. But we must not do anything that would make them want us to leave. Tasmania must always be our home, Jassim. There is nowhere else for us to go.'

'Will the rest of our family come here from Iraq one day?'

'I don't know, I don't know,' she answered, shaking her head and looking distraught. 'Tell me, Jassim, why do you think people here like war?'

He picked up his school bag and took out a sheet of paper filled with

notes. 'Today, on the front page of the newspaper, it said, "War in Iraq –
an eight-page special." Something that is special is something people like.'

'Yes. Though I cannot believe people here or anywhere would like
war.' Her eyes toured the lounge room. 'All right, this is what we can do
for our English work tonight,' she said. 'We'll look up the word "special"
in our English dictionary, then try to work out why it was used like
that. And if you accidentally…' she paused to let her big eyes bore into
him '…accidentally see other things about Iraq in newspapers at school
that trouble you, write them down and bring them home to me. We'll
look the words up and learn about them together. But remember, this is
just for you to share with me, and no one else, Jassim. Especially don't
say anything to your father. He thinks that by reading the newspapers,
or watching the news about Iraq on television, his children will suffer
unnecessarily. And more than anything,' she enunciated slowly, 'he does
not want that to happen.'

'I know, Mama. But at school Ms Roberts sometimes says to us, "You
can't bury your head in the sand."'

'Yes.' Memory kindled a smile. 'There is that expression about sandy
heads in Iraq too, where there is so much sand to do that in… But now,
for doing so well in reciting the hadith, there's a prize for you in the fridge.
It has a green frog on it.'

***

'"It's show time for Franks." Then on the second line it says, "Timid
Tommy has taken over where Stormin' Norman left off."'

'So what words are not so good for you?' his mother asked in English.

'Show time.' Jassim took a sheet of headline words out of his school
bag. 'Don't be upset, Mama, but I just couldn't help asking Ms Roberts
for help.'

His mother put her chin in her hand and propped her elbow on the
table. A reassuring smile brightened her face. 'That's what a teacher is for,
Jassim. So, what did she say?'

He consulted his notes. 'Timid Tommy Franks and Stormin'

Norman are just strange names of American army generals, so they're not important. But "show time" means entertainment, or having a good time, like at a circus or somewhere where there's a stage and singers sing and people play music.'

'I cannot understand how that is right, Jassim. I must get the dictionary,' she said, standing up.

They were still reading the dictionary and discussing the many meanings of show time when headlights beamed in through the window and a taxi swept up the driveway.

'Oh, is it really so late?' his mother exclaimed, hopping up. She slapped the dictionary closed and quickly cleared the table. 'Don't worry about your prayer mat, Jassim. Pray in bed now, now, now.'

***

'"Bombs rain down on Baghdad" and, Mama, below those words was a large picture of bright yellow balls, like small suns, dropping out of the sky on the buildings there.'

Her pose had changed the past few days. Now she sat there weary-eyed, with her hands clasped tightly in front of her. 'Is it the words or the picture that trouble you?' Her eyes found objects, other than him, to focus on.

'Everything, Mama, but...but that word "rain".'

She got up automatically and went over to the bookshelf for the dictionary.

'No, I don't need that,' he said. He wadded up his paper and dropped it in his bag. 'Rain brings life, Mama. Bombs kill life. Why would those two words be used together?'

'I don't know, I don't know,' she answered, returning to the table. 'Maybe for tonight you should just do your school work until prayer time.'

***

'"When Mom Goes to War – a family tale. This American helicopter pilot and her husband are now based in Kuwait, leaving behind their fourteen-year-old daughter.'"

She eyed her son curiously. 'Was that from an Australian newspaper?'

'Not a newspaper, a magazine.'

'That you accidentally saw at school?'

'It's just that the cover had this close-up face of a pretty lady on it. She was wearing a helmet, and had sunglasses and lipstick on. I just couldn't help looking at her, and then the writing.'

'Her first and then the writing. I see. What is it we should talk about, then?'

'I've looked up the word "tale" at school. It's a story, Mama. So it's a family story about a mother who leaves her child to fly a helicopter from Kuwait to Iraq to drop bombs like rain because it's show time and war in Iraq is special.' Tears sprang to his eyes.

She moved next to him and hugged and rocked him in her arms. 'Today, Jassim, I watched the news on television,' she said, reverting to Arabic. 'They showed bombs and missiles falling on Baghdad like rain. Next they showed the American president making a speech. Much of what he said I couldn't understand, either because I did not know the words or, if I did know them, they made no sense to me.' Holding on to her son with one arm, she reached into her dress pocket and took out her own piece of paper. 'I have here a word he used often. It's called "liberate". I looked the word up in the dictionary. It means to bring freedom. So I ask myself, how are we to understand that dropping bombs and missiles like rain on people is meant to bring life and freedom?'

'I don't know,' he answered, burrowing into her arms.

'You see, I'm as confused as you are. Do you know what I think, Jassim?' she asked rhetorically. 'I think your father is right. We should stick to reading the Koran and your schoolbooks, and not read newspapers or magazines or watch the television to try to understand what is happening in Iraq. It only brings more confusion and pain.'

Jassim pulled away. 'So we keep our heads in the sand, then, Mama?'

'I think so. Surely our heads won't be the only ones in there.'

Fishing Manhattan

It was his longest cast for the day, probably his longest one ever, and when the sinker 'plonked', sending ripples across the mirror-calm sea, Billy felt a buzz of satisfaction. He let the line run off his reel until the sinker hit the bottom, then wound up the slack and sat in his fold-up chair.

'Good boy,' his grandad said, all shrunken up and sick next to him. He put a hand on Billy's wrist. 'You know, Billy, there are certain sounds in life, like there are images, I carry around with me. The sound of a sinker hitting the water like that has long been one of them.' He bent down and gave Jonah a pat, which sent his dog back to sleep.

It was hard for Billy to know whether he should encourage his grandad to talk or not. His mother had just said, 'He wants to watch you fish. He's got his medication, but if he has a bad turn, ring me on the mobile. Otherwise, I'll visit your sister in town, go to the supermarket and be back in a couple of hours to pick you up.'

'The plonk of a sinker always carried better in autumn when I was a boy fishing on the Manhattan Beach pier,' his granddad continued, 'like it does here on this quiet old jetty.' He took off his sunglasses and squinted across the water, then went on with a story he'd told Billy versions of before. 'I was still in nappies when my parents busted up. My father fled Los Angeles for the Alaskan wilderness, never to return, while my mother and I went to live with my grandmother. My earliest memory of that place is of waking up on a still night…just after I'd started school in autumn it was, and hearing the fog horn bellowing like a great sea cow and knowing that its number one sound conductor, the fog, would be thick in the morning.' A smile stretched his face. His eyes were suddenly full of life. 'On weekends, I'd get up at first grey light and sneak into the lounge room, which often smelled of stale cigarettes, and was full of half-empty beer glasses and people sleeping and snoring in lounge chairs. At the age of five, or maybe it was six, I took my first unassisted drink of beer out of one of those glasses. It amused my grandmother so much when her eyes opened that she decided to polish off a glass of beer with me.' His laugh was a wheeze, like his windpipe had cracked.

A car dragging an aluminium dinghy came down the ramp. They watched two men get out and launch the boat, before parking the car and motoring off towards Bruny Island, rising like the hump of a whale on the near horizon.

'You're eleven, aren't you, Billy?' His grandad asked, out of the blue.

Billy looked at him quizzically. A few weeks earlier, he'd have known without doubt. 'Twelve in two weeks, Grandad.'

He smiled. 'You needn't be so anxious to add on the years. Life's here to do that for us without any help.' He paused and squinted. 'We were talking about something else earlier, weren't we?'

'You drinking beer in Manhattan with your grandmum.'

'Ah, yes. The picture's coming back… Anyway, Billy, it wasn't long before I was walking to the Manhattan pier every Saturday and Sunday morning – fishing rod in one hand, tackle box in the other. The beach areas weren't built up then, so there were still plenty of sand dunes to cross to get there. And in those days, nobody gave a thought to the dangers grade one kids might encounter walking long distances to get out on that pier and fish for the day.'

The sound of the dinghy's outboard merged with a small plane flying up the channel.

'So you never got lost, Grandad, not even in the fog?'

'Never did. I could smell the sea, and I knew the area as well as I knew my own bedroom. When I got there, the sounds directed me: the muffled voices of old men on slat benches, the squawking seagulls perched on the railings and the hum of cars up on the main road.' His smile came again. 'And of course sinkers hitting the water with a plonk.' He watched the small plane veer west towards Hobart before his eyes settled on the sea again. 'It was illegal to overhead cast there, so I had to lean over the railing and swing my line under the pier, then out over the water. The heavier the sinker, the farther the cast, and the better the chance of catching a big one. It was a good thing the water was surfer-free when the fog was in.'

'What sort of bait did you use?'

'The place was full of fish in those days. So it depended on what you were fishing for. The biggest prize of all was a barn door halibut – like a giant flounder, big enough to carpet your bedroom. For trying to catch one of those, people bought live anchovies netted the night before and brought in on Grisly Garibaldi's bait boat.' He chuckled and coughed.

'Hard to forget a name like that, isn't it? It was well earned, though. Garibaldi was a miserable sod. A perennial wooden-spooner in the happiness stakes. Everything about him seemed to stoop and droop, like the weight of the world was on him. His heavy eyes were the colour of ripe tomatoes. He had a long face and a beard like black wool… Geez, the spats he and old Jonesy in the kiosk used to get into – about nothing really. Rose, Jonesy's wife, would fire up as well, separating them and blistering their ears before yanking Jonesy back into the kiosk. If they'd sold tickets, they could've retired… Rose always watched out for me. There was always an extra hook or sinker stored under the counter if she heard I'd lost mine, or a sandwich that needed to be eaten, or milk that was due to go off in the next two seconds if I didn't drink it. Jonesy and Rose never had any kids. A pity, really.' He reached down, patted Jonah and watched the sea. 'Anyway, where was I?'

'Baiting your hook for halibut, Grandad.'

'Right. I've strayed a bit, haven't I? A proper halibut rig was an arm's length leader and a number four hook tied just above the sinker. Halibut ignored anchovy heads like they were poison, so the trick was to hook an anchovy through its gill slit and back under its skin, without disturbing the gills. It required the patience and deft touch of a surgeon… In this accelerating world of ours, I've always thought *Halibut Fishing As a Life Skill* would make an excellent book title.' His coughing started up again. 'Anyway, after casting my line out – plonk – there was little to do but sit and wait and be patient. On those foggy mornings, I'd listen to the foghorn moan and time how long it took for the sun to burn through. Seagulls got active when it did. But the old men, with nowhere else to go, always stayed the same – nattering away in slow voices, their eyes screwed up against the brightening sea and sky. Nowadays, of course, the live anchovies are gone. So are the halibut… Still, we'll need to get back there, you and me, and do some fishing before their autumn ends.'

***

In the thick fog, they kept the traffic sounds behind them and used the occasional footsteps and silhouettes of passers-by to gauge where they were going. When Billy heard the cry of a seagull and started catching scraps of muted conversation, he thought how both strange and familiar the pier was to him. Fog and the accents were new; but only three weeks had passed since his grandad last talked about fishing here, and he had pictured the place would be like this.

'Did you know there'd be fog, Mum?' he asked.

'I was fairly certain. I rang your Aunt Claudia and asked her to keep an eye on the long-range weather forecast here. She went one better and contacted a man in the weather bureau, then used her considerable charm to stay in contact with him. When she rang home and gave me today's forecast, I knew two late seats on Qantas wouldn't come at discount prices, but then this was never going to be a discount holiday, was it?'

'No.' More fog-hidden gulls squawked. 'I reckon we're over water now.'

'Good. I'll hold on to your arm while you find us a spot. Got your line rigged up?'

He hadn't fished since his last day with his grandad. 'Yes.'

They found an empty slat bench and Billy set his pole up against the railing. He opened his tackle box, took out a knife and sliced open the bag of salted anchovies. While he concentrated on baiting his hook, his mother edged away until she couldn't see him. She reached into her daypack and took out a small urn. 'Let me know when you're about to cast your line out, okay?' Her voice cracked with emotion.

His warning came seconds later.

She tipped the urn and its contents spilled out – grey on grey – before a 'plonk' sounded somewhere out there on the water.

They sat together on the bench and listened for the foghorn, but it never sounded. After a while, a beam of sunlight showed. They watched it probe, retreat, probe again and grow – thinning and swirling and lifting sections of fog so that the sea first appeared as bits of gauzy, leaden patches. Those patches stretched and brightened until the entire sea was exposed, still and sun-streaked below.

A breeze crept through and the sea began to move towards shore, lapping down. Seagulls lifted their cries and took off – skimming and rising and banking over the water. Aircraft from the nearby airport did the same, while the rumble of traffic on the main road intensified.

A couple in leather pants and boots, their hands gripped to each other's backsides, moved unsteadily down the pier towards them. The bloke's voice rang out, 'Shitfire, baby. See them great steel birds soarin' up out there, heaven-bound? It's flight time. So shake your sexy caboose and let's join 'em! Remount Big Monte and hold on ta your panties.'

'Won't have ta, Jay-boy. I forgot ta put 'em on.'

'Hot damn. You're sauce ta my turnip, girlfriend! You know how much I'm lovin' ya, don't ya?'

'Love's a many splendoured thing…'specially now.'

'Poetry.'

They lurched to a stop, just metres away. Nipples like rocks against her pink, skin-tight skivy, the girl reached up on tiptoed boots and wrapped her arms around the bloke's neck. Her thin, pale face poked out of a mass of blonde curls.

'That look, Jay-boy – hungry, like I'm top of the menu again.'

'Never a time when you won't be.'

'You sweet, sweet boy. Come 'ere. I've got your entrée for ya.'

She kissed him in a way Billy had never seen anyone kissed before. He turned away, stunned they could do that in full view. He concentrated on the beach to his left that stretched up to a mass of housing without breaks or evidence of past sand dunes. Another pier showed on the far horizon, perhaps three or four kilometres away.

'A friendly pair of fishermen.' his mum said, unruffled, minutes later. 'Or do you reckon they work for the local tourist council?'

Billy looked around to ensure they'd gone. 'Yeah, right, Mum.'

From the car park, a motorcycle – obviously Big Monte – chug-started then amplified to the level of a log truck spitting gunfire exhaust. Seconds later, Big Monte rocketed up the road towards town, slowing cars and scattering people.

'Bye-bye Baby and Jay-boy,' his mother said, wrapping an arm around Billy's waist and watching the ocean with him. 'Do keep an eye out for low-flying power poles.'

Billy giggled gratefully. 'Love you, Mum,' he said.

She laid her head on his shoulder. 'There's no greater poetry than that, Billy.' Half a minute later, she looked up the pier. 'Fancy a walk out to the end? The fish aren't exactly fighting for our attention here.'

'People aren't either, now. There's nobody around.'

'No. Still, if the normal clientele is anything like what's just gone past, we won't suffer from being on our own.'

They walked.

A concrete rotunda, shaped like a war zone observation post, stood near the end of the pier. Its tiled roof was layered in bird droppings, its door and windows boarded up and graffiti-filled. This had to be the kiosk his grandad told him about. On the left, where the railing began to turn outwards, was another much smaller building. It was boarded up too. A sign hung over the padlocked door. Billy took a closer look at it and could just make out the words – BAIT SHOP.

He stepped back beside his mother. 'So, Mum, right here is where tickets could've been sold to watch Jonesy and Grisly Garibaldi argue.'

'Is it? I wouldn't know. What did they argue about?'

Her not knowing surprised him. As they continued, rounding the rotunda, he told her the story.

The breeze picked up, blowing two sachets from under a far bench towards the rotunda, where an old man – a bundle of grime with matted white hair and a beard – slept on his side. A ragged blanket covered his legs, a rolled up newspaper served as his pillow.

They veered away from the man and walked towards the bench, but stopped when they saw a syringe dangling from the top slat, its needle buried in the wood. 'You reckon Baby and Jay-boy left something behind, Mum?'

'More than likely,' she answered, losing her brightness.

They avoided the bench and went over to the railing, picking up the heavy smells of oil from a refinery up the coast. As they stood there, departing aircraft banked over in thirty-second intervals, the sweeping whines forcing them to cover their ears.

Someone tapped Billy's shoulder. He swung round, startled, and viewed a bony-faced figure staring down at him.

The man extended a cupped hand close to his face. 'Coffee money,' he rasped, his breath sour, his clothes reeking of dirt and sweat. He used his other hand to scratch the bristle around his neck and gather his worn overcoat around him.

Billy's mother took out some coins and gave them to the man. But his hand stayed.

'Two coffees. One for my friend,' he demanded.

Two others like him rounded the rotunda, ogling the sleeper first, then looking their way. Billy had no idea where they came from.

'Go, Billy,' his mother said, pushing him away.

He reached back and grabbed her hand and they broke into a jog the men had no hope of matching.

Back at their bench, Billy reeled his line in fast. 'If Grandad had to die when he did,' he said, 'then I'm glad we didn't come back here first, like he wanted us to.'

Her arm found his waist again, her head his shoulder. 'You're right. Memories of places are best left undisturbed. Things change. This pier is a very different place now.'

Billy was ready to go. 'What now, Mum?'

She looked at her watch. 'Hungry?'

'Yeah, I am. Why don't we ring up Aunt Claudia at work and ask her to meet us somewhere for lunch?'

'What a good idea. Somewhere that has more than one item on the menu.'

Billy could smile about that now. 'Whatever's at the top is what I'm going for.'

'Pig's bum, you are.'

***

'Plonk.' Fifth cast in succession, each one a bit further than the last. Good boy, he heard his grandad say in his mind. Fishing wasn't important for him now, only his casting distance was, and the sound his sinker made hitting the water. In the calm conditions, nothing rivalled that 'plonk' for volume, although a small boat was putt-putting towards Bruny Island and seagulls on either side of the jetty stalked the shoreline – a couple of them vocally.

Billy reeled in his line, heaved his rod back over his shoulder and let fly again. 'Plonk.' No words came from his grandad this time, as the cast was his shortest one for the day. A stab of loneliness hit him. He'd never been out here alone before. When he got to his grandad's age, he'd have no stories of Jonesy, Rose or Grisly Garibaldi types to tell anyone. Though there'd always be grandad to talk about, and that was probably enough. Time to start fishing, he decided. He let his sinker drop to the bottom and sat next to Jonah, already stretched out on his new dog cushion.

He looked over where his grandad sat that last day and recalled what they'd talked about. 'Fishing Manhattan was all right,' Billy said to him, stretching the truth. 'Things change though, Grandad. I like fishing here more.'

Jonah slept. A seagull wheeled over, and minutes later Billy felt a fish – most likely a flathead – taking an interest in his bait. 'Be patient, Billy,' he recalled his grandad saying. 'Good, good. That's it. That's it. Now set the hook.'

Billy pulled his rod back sharply. It was no halibut on the line, but it would do. 'Flathead fishing as a life skill,' Billy remarked. Tears came. So did a smile. 'Thanks, Grandad.'

www.ingramcontent.com/pod-product-compliance
Lightning Source LLC
Chambersburg PA
CBHW071541100726

47908CB00004B/1466